HOW
YOU
LEFT ME

Cienna Collins

AJC Publishing
PO Box 8050
Oakleigh East Vic 3166 Australia
E: aj@ajcpublishing.com.au
W: www.ajcpublishing.com.au

978-1-7637190-2-6 Print
978-1-7637190-3-3 Ebook
978-1-7637190-4-0 Audiobook

Interior design by AJC Publishing
Cover design by GetCovers
Image licensing: Depositphotos
Typeset in Garamond 12
Printed and bound by IngramSpark

Edition 2 published 2024
Edition 1 published 2020 as Oleanders Are Poisonous by AJ Collins

Also by Cienna Collins

How You Left Me (Part 1)
How You Found Me (Part 2)
The Disappearing Season

Praise For How You Left Me

Collins expertly guides us through Lauren's brutal, complicated coming of age in a poignant tale about growing up too fast, forgiving too slowly, and the healing power of love, friendship, and family - however it comes.

- Nicole Hayes, author of The Whole of My World, One True thing and A Shadow's Breath

From the first pages, Collins breathes life into her characters, fuels your need to know more. With empathy and insight, she sheds light on the dark experiences of life, shows the power of connection and the courage it takes to move on. A big-hearted coming of age novel about love and trust and everything that comes between.

- Melissa Manning, author of Smokehouse Collection

Author's Note

Content warning: References to sexual abuse, mental health, suicide, self-harm, homophobia.

Grammar note: This book uses Australian spelling and grammar conventions.

From the author: While I have experienced some of the issues explored in this work, the character of Lauren is not me. All the characters depicted in this book are fictional. The story is, however, based on a kernel of murky truth, which has lain simmering within me for years, and like the stone within Lauren, it needed to see daylight.

I hope that each of my books will entertain and move you, that each is an act of escapism, a moment to step away from your everyday life, pause and introspect.

For Mr Bunny
It was always going to be

Vulnerability is a journey to destiny

One stole her innocence
One stole her heart
One gave her hope
And the secret awoke

1

Catalyst

The cogs are turning in Harry's head. I can tell by the way he looks up and to the left, as if he's searching the ceiling of the bus for something his memory has stored there.

"A-E-S-T-H-E-T-I-C-I-S-M."

"Damn!"

I hand over his prize – the second for this bus ride – but he pushes it back at me. "Nah, you keep it. It was too easy."

"Was not! Take it."

Usually, I'd be ahead by at least three Chupa Chups, but lately my head hasn't been in the game. I sigh and look out as we pass canola crops holding their own in the stinking afternoon heat, their blooms bright as the daffodils Mum used to grow. Before.

As if he's read my mind, Harry leans in and whispers, "How's things at home?"

I squeeze my hands together, unsure if it's my memory or his closeness that's made me tense. I focus on the red vinyl of the seat in front of me; the stitching is coming loose, unravelling, like my family. "It is what it is."

He's silent for a while, then says, "Mum and Dad are always asking. They'd like to help."

"Yeah, I know. Thanks."

Harry's parents, the Carters, are into voluntourism – volunteering holidays. Always helping. It's what they do. But they can't help us.

"Sorry, kiddo." He bumps my shoulder, then grins when I give him a dirty look; he knows I hate it when he calls me that. Just because he's a year above me, doesn't make him an adult. He's done it since I was eleven, when he took me under his wing as part of the headmaster's first-year mentorship program. I was the youngest in my class, since I skipped a grade, thanks to Mum's home schooling. "Bright for my age' they called me – not so great when all the just-turned-teens think of you as a kid. I was supposed to be allocated a girl mentor, but that year they were short. I'm glad. So, so glad. But I'd never tell Harry that.

"Get stuffed."

"Fork you."

I have to work really, really hard not to smile; we've both been watching *The Good Place* on Netflix. The swearing references are killer funny.

The bus slows, close to Harry's farm, and he leans down, shaggy hair falling across his face as he sticks his Chupa Chups into his backpack. He stands, towering above me, then shoves his pack over his shoulder.

"Hey, mopey face. You coming over Sunday for a jam? Got a surprise for you."

I pretend to think about it – as if I'd actually consider saying no to spending time with him, even if my scratching around on vocals doesn't measure up to his guitar or piano finesse – he's one of those multi-talented virtuosos you love to hate.

"What sort of surprise?"

He pulls a you'll-have-to-wait face.

I try for nonchalance. "Yeah, okay. Probably late afternoon. Got some chores first."

"Fair enough. Whenever you're ready. See ya ... *kiddo*."

I flip him off, but he's already turned away. When he's outside, I slide the window open and call out. "Hang on to those Chupa Chups for Sunday. I'm winning them back."

He turns and waves while the bus carries me forwards. Now that there's distance between us, I relax, daydream. I imagine him waving like a soldier going off to fight in a war, and me, a nurse, heading off to help the wounded ... only the wounded is Mum.

I sag. Once, soft rounded edges and tight hugs, now she's all angles and confusion. No. I'm not going there. I shake it off and reach for my backpack. Twenty minutes of travel is twenty minutes I can study and keep my mind busy. Or find new words to challenge Harry.

A hint of red lolly wrapper is sticking out of the front pocket of my backpack. "Harry! I said I didn't want it."

What will I do next year after he graduates and goes into the mythical "real world" our teachers are always on about? What will I do if he meets someone serious before I'm brave enough to tell him how I feel? Samuel has this old record on vinyl by this band, Smokers or Smoky or something. There's a song on it, "Living next door to Alice", about a guy who never gets the chance to tell the girl next door he loves her. I have nightmares about being that loser.

I should tell him. Maybe I will. This Sunday. But how will he react? What if I stuff everything up? Or worse, what if he laughs?

The bus pulls up near the post office, and I drag myself out of my seat. Bill, the driver, slides a pack of roll-your-owns from his pocket and climbs down in front of me. He'll be heading across the road to put in his regular Friday fish and chips order. I turn in the opposite direction, and passing the pub, I notice a "Help Wanted" sign in the window. It'd be good to have a job over the Christmas break, earn a bit of money. Even better, it would get me out of the house more. Pity I'm not legal yet.

Our whole street seems to be sagging from the heat. Mary Worthington, one of our neighbours, is pulling her granny trolley along the lumpy footpath. Her huffing carries from three houses away as she approaches, her bloated ankles pouring over the top of her shoes like warm, droopy candle wax. She must be so uncomfortable. How does she cope in this weather?

She catches sight of me and waves. "Lauren!"

Damn. I'll have to wait. Either that or pretend I haven't seen her. No, I can't do that. Mary's a kind sort, and besides, she's Harry's gran, so that's a good reason not to be rude. It's just so freakin' *hot*.

I slump against our fence under the shade of the oleander with its almost-deadly blossoms. I always think of them that way because, when I was little, Mum caught me stuffing the poisonous frilly flowers in my mouth. She nearly had a heart attack. I expect my child brain thought the hot pink blooms looked like lollies. I vomited a lot and wasn't too good for a couple of days, but hey, I'm still here. I doubt she'd notice them these days. Whatever – they smell nice, and the tree is keeping the cruel sun off me.

"Here you go, love." Mary holds out a sheet of paper – the latest Ladies Auxiliary newsletter. It's covered in photos of who won the latest bowls competition and other boring small-town pap. "Give it to your mum for me, will you? I'd come in, but I've got to get the ice cream in the freezer before we have to suck it up through a straw."

"Okay." If I keep my answers short, hopefully she'll move on, and both of us can get some relief. That and Samuel is adamant we shouldn't be sharing anything with people. "NTK" he calls it in cop-speak: need to know basis. I guess he doesn't think of the council nurses who look after Mum on weekdays as "people".

Mary has sweat rivulets running down her forehead and into her eyes. She squints and blinks a few times. "How is she?"

"Okay."

"Well, yell out if you or Samuel need any help, alright? She's welcome over at my place anytime if you want a break. You know that, yes?"

I nod.

"Good girl." She shuffles off across the road to her house, two doors down.

I creak open our front gate and trudge up the gravel, pulling at the damp collar of my school dress. A dizzy haze is coming off our corrugated roof. The tree leaning over our veranda looks pretty with its pink peppercorns drooping in grape-like bunches, but it's doing nothing to ward off the heat. Days like this, even the shade is unbearable. Geez, it's only early September. Summer is going to be hell. Yay for the Mallee. Once the weather clicks over, it's freakin' hot one day, dust and spit the next.

I dump my school bag inside my bedroom doorway and head to the kitchen. Mary's mention of ice cream has me craving an icy pole.

Good. Mum and Samuel are out. Bliss to have the place to myself for a while. They must have kept the blinds down all day, and the air conditioner is quietly buzzing overhead – instant heaven. I open the freezer. Inside are four stacks of meticulously folded socks.

2

Ineluctable

Samuel is up before five o'clock, knocking about the house like a blowfly. He'll be trying to find stuff to keep himself busy: cleaning up last night's teacups, turning on the washing machine, cutting the kettle whistle short before it reaches its shrill peak. The back door slams, and I picture him outside, watering the tomatoes, letting the chooks out for a while – things he would normally do in the evening, after work, after dinner when it's cooler.

He wouldn't have slept much last night; it's Saturday, the day we get Mum's final test results. I don't see the point. The answer is obvious.

I pull on my dressing gown and head down the hallway to the bathroom. The door is open and Mum's in there, standing at the sink in her nightgown, staring into the vanity mirror. She's so focused on her reflection, her hand paused mid-air with a brush, she doesn't notice me. I watch as her blank expression becomes lucid. She frowns.

"I told you, no," she says to her reflection. "You can't take it." She threatens the mirror with her brush, raises her voice. "Rob needs it. How the heck do you expect us to manage without it? Stop coming around here." She's yelling now.

"Leave us alone. Go on!" She throws the brush at the mirror. I flinch, expecting a shatter, but the brush clatters harmlessly into the sink.

Oh god. I want to skulk away, pretend I haven't seen, avoid her like a cat skirts a dog on a chain. Not that Mum's a dog; she's great... *was*.

She leans on the basin, closes her eyes. "It's Rob's. I've told that man a million times. He should get his own."

"Mum?"

She opens her eyes. Blinks. "What?" She sounds vague, as if she's just woken.

"Who are you talking to?"

She turns to me, long dark hair falling over her face. "Christopher."

"Christopher? Your old boss at the bakery?"

"No, no. From the Hill's property. He wants to buy your father's tractor. He keeps asking."

I bite back the sharp stab in my heart. *Dad*. "The farm's gone, Mum. We sold it."

"Everything okay?" It's Samuel. I turn to look down the hall. He's peering through the back door flyscreen.

I raise a hand. "We're fine."

"I won't be long," he says. "Put the kettle on?"

"Okay."

Mum's looking at me, hard, brain trying to process. She turns back to the mirror, eyes widening as if she's surprised to see her own reflection. She looks down, picks up the brush, then smiles at me.

"Come, my cherub."

She sits on the edge of the bath and beckons. I step towards her, then turn around and kneel on the bathmat in front of her, letting her stroke the brush through my hair – so much like hers, maybe a touch wavier – letting her take me back with her, to another bathroom, another house, before we lived with Samuel, before Dad died, before she lost her mind.

I picture myself, a five-year-old, arguing over her wanting to get the knots out of my unruly hair, then plait it into stupid pigtails, when all I want is to hurry outside to ride the new bike Dad has bought for my birthday. I don't care if the yard is still muddy from recent rain; I'm eager to plonk Madam Puff, our red bantam chicken, into my bike's wicker basket and ride us around as if we're in a best-in-show parade.

"Will you stop wriggling?" she says to my young self.

"Ow!"

"Five minutes. Then you can dab a little of my perfume. Okay?"

I sulkily nod, and though my heart sings at the thought of rose-scented wrists, I grimace while she pulls as gently as she can.

Now, ten years on, I'd let her brush my hair forever if I could have her back. She strokes and smooths, strokes and smooths, humming as she works. I close my eyes, drift, can almost smell the sweet roses. She doesn't think to wear the fragrance anymore. So many things are lost to her. And me.

She stops and taps my shoulder. "Up, up."

I stand, and she puts her hands on my waist, turning me to face her, then cups my chin, smiling sadly. "You better get dressed, darling. We've got the doctor's soon."

My throat catches. *Mum.* How does she do that? Move seamlessly from fairyland to reality in a breath? I wish she'd just go or stay. It's a callous, terrible thought, but this back and forth makes me want to scream. Why can't she just be Mum?

She stands and shuffles past, heading to her and Samuel's bedroom. I leave her to puzzle over the monumental choice of what colour scarf to bring today.

A few minutes on, I'm sitting sticky-fingered at the kitchen table, trying to fill the hole where my heart should be with toast and honey. Samuel comes in from the garden and sits, slips his big hands around the mug of tea I've made him. His hair is so short it might as well be shaven – a hangover from his early years in the police force. Spell *fastidious*. In our town, people probably wouldn't care if he turned up for his shift in jeans and a flannel shirt, but he never would. It's uniforms all the way.

Rules are rules.

It took me forever to learn this, to keep my mouth shut around Samuel, to accept that he likes to lay down the law at home as well as at work.

"It's only a bloody window," I yelled, ten years old and full of rage because living with him the past two years didn't make him my father, and he shouldn't have been bossing me around, even if he was going to marry my mum.

"You watch your mouth, young lady."

"No! You watch yours."

"I know you've been through a tough time, but that's no excuse to be churlish to your elders."

I laughed then, more out of fear than *churlishness*, whatever that meant. "Elders? What are you, a church minister?"

I was pushing it, but I couldn't stop myself. I didn't break the window on purpose, did I?

He rounded on me with his height and bulk, and I backed down. When he lowered his voice to a growl, it scared me even more. "That's enough. You're ten, not two. It's time you learnt to act your age. Just because you have a roof over your head now, doesn't mean you'll have one tomorrow."

"Will so," I whispered behind his back, as he left me to ponder what he meant. I hadn't liked the sound of whatever it was. Was he going to chuck me out and keep my mum? Send me to boarding school?

Okay, it was over five years ago, and I'd copped several smacks to the back of my legs with a wooden spoon before I succumbed, but he never mentioned it again. Still, words like that stay with you.

Samuel slumps in his chair. "I can't do this," he says, hands knitting into a cap over his head. I pause, toast halfway to my mouth. Samuel's voice sounds as if it's struggling to escape, tense, like water trapped in a folded hose. This indestructible bull of a man, this six-foot-something copper who always takes care of everyone else's troubles, actually needs someone to lean on?

The pain on his face tells me how much he loves my mum. "Samuel? Do you want me to come with you?" I really hope he says no. *Please.* I don't know how to handle this either.

He's buried in his own thoughts. "I'm not letting her go."

A string of honey leaks from my toast onto my plate. I wipe at the puddle with my finger, then suck on it. Samuel looks up, absently watching my motions. His eyes have a faraway look in them, but I suddenly feel weird, my finger in my mouth like that. Ever since my boobs decided to put in a late appearance – poof! A sudden growth spurt, literally overnight, I swear – they've made me self-conscious, mostly because of the ogling from boys at school. Not that Samuel had ever, would ever, look at me that way. God, no. I'm lucky to get a hug from him. Even then it's one quick squeeze, then his hands grasp my arms, ready to push me away again. An army sergeant embrace. Or cop, in his case.

The lounge room clock chimes eight times. I drop my toast and sigh. "Okay. Give me a minute to brush my teeth and get dressed."

⸻◆⸻

Inside the entrance to the hospital clinic, a table is laid out with stuff made or donated by the Ladies Auxiliary: packets of coconut-covered rum balls – are they allowed to sell stuff with alcohol in them here? Or are they like the ones Mum used to make for me, without rum? And why not just call them coconut balls, or chocolate balls? – a multi-coloured tea cosy, notepads, crocheted baby booties in soft pinks and yellows, other bits and pieces nobody wants. A note is sticky-taped to a bank-issued money tin: "Honesty Box".

Mum hangs back to pick up a knitted clothes hanger that's fallen onto the linoleum. She used to be crazy about knitting. *Crazy.* Poor word choice. I still have some of the jumpers, beanies and scarves she made with love – if not taste. Now all of her knitting morphs into some weirdly knotted mass, which looks like the mould that grows near the back fence after we've had a few wet days in a row.

"Not as good as mine," she declares loudly, waving the hanger.

"Put it back, Delia," Samuel says. I know he doesn't mean to be harsh; he's tense.

Mum obeys, and he drags her away by the hand.

The waiting room is stark with its easy-to-clean chairs, floors and walls. As we sit, Samuel's denials continue. "You're okay. We're okay. We can manage." He pats Mum's hand, then holds it tight in his fist. I'm not sure if he's talking to himself, or to me, or to Mum, so I keep quiet, my heart constricting for his pain. Our pain. I want to say something supportive, to tell him it isn't all that bad, but the socks in the freezer, the oven mitt in the toaster and the hairdryer left blowing hotter and hotter on the bathroom sink, won't let me. Enough denial. I'm secretly glad the months of tests have come to an end.

The doctor takes us into his office and swivels his computer monitor so we can see. He points to grey and white scans of Mum's brain. "See these areas here?" he says. I peer closely, but all I see are squiggles. "I'm afraid the progression has sped up."

Samuel and I look to see Mum's reaction. She sits stiff and upright as if she's in Sunday church, a slight upward tilt to her mouth. Is she smiling? Maybe she isn't listening.

I try to catch Samuel's eye, hoping he might break through to her. He pats her hand again. He's still holding on tight, as if letting go will send her floating off into the awful world he's trying to keep her from. "Delia, did you hear what the doctor said?"

"Yes, I did." She pats him back as if he's the one being given the bad news. "I might be losing my memory, but I'm not deaf."

The doctor continues, using words like hippocampus, plaques, atrophied. Though he explains them, the words flow through me and slip away. What's wrong with me? I should be paying attention. Remembering.

"What are our options? How do we fix this?" Samuel asks, as if he hasn't asked it too many times before.

The doctor looks at Mum, who's busy playing with her scarf, then lowers his voice to Samuel. "Maybe I can give you a call? Talk privately?"

Samuel shakes his head. "We're not hiding anything from Delia. She needs to know too."

"Yes, but—"

Samuel glares.

The doctor sighs. "Okay. Well, research is ongoing, but there's no cure, as you know." He explains, again, how variable it is. "Is she becoming disorientated? Volatile?"

Hell, yes! I want to say. But I don't. How does Mum feel being spoken about as if she's not even here?

"She's fine," Samuel says, and I flick him an incredulous look. *She's not.*

"If she does, medication may help manage her behaviour, but you probably need to start thinking about a future care plan." He holds out some pamphlets. "I know you already have home assistance, but you might want to think about'—he glances at Mum again.—"Sorry, Delia ... a plan for when things get unmanageable."

Samuel ignores the pamphlets, anger edging his voice. "I said she's fine. Not a burden." He stands. "We'll manage."

In the car, on the way home, false bravado hangs like dirty laundry no-one wants to air.

"We need to go to the chemist," Samuel says. Then he talks about buying fertiliser for the vegetable patch and picking up milk.

Mum nods, agreeable, smiling.

I struggle to find the right words, ones that won't tip things into anger or upset. I want to shake them both, make them tell me what we're going to do. *How* we're going manage. The doctor seems to think things are going to get worse. When? And what does worse look like?

I should have said something earlier, back when I knew things weren't right. Before Samuel came along. People said it was grief over Dad. The flaky, airy-fairy-ness of her. I sometimes wondered if it was caused by having me so late in life. "I was a young forty-two," Mum had said. "But they had to resuscitate me after you were born." Did something happen to her brain then? I don't even know why she told me that. It gave me nightmares.

Still, I was right, wasn't I? "Early-onset dementia" the doctor called it. Not some twenty-six-letter-long disease none of us could pronounce. Just dementia. Plain and simple. He couldn't say when it started, but I knew.

⸻ ⸱◦⸱ ⸻

After lunch, Samuel and I stand side by side doing the dishes. I'm a bit squirrely because there's something I need to ask him. Something personal, and I'm not sure if now is the right time, given what we've been through this morning. What the hell, I take a breath—

And Mum interrupts. "It's not the way it's done, is it?"

I glance at her. She's sitting at the kitchen table flicking through magazines and holding a mumbled conversation with herself, or maybe invisible friends.

She says it again, louder.

I frown. Is she talking to us? "What's that, Mum?"

She looks up. "The papers. They don't get folded that way, do they?"

I put the tea towel down, then go to look over her shoulder at the open magazine. I can't see what she's talking about. "What papers, Mum?"

"Not that!" She slaps her open palm down on the magazine. I step back. "The other day. The papers on the thing. *You know.*"

I bite my lip. "No, I don't know. Where was the thing?" I ask, trying to fathom a clue.

"Yes," she insists, irritated. "The other day. On the thing by the ... the ..." She stares mid-air, brow furrowed.

Samuel has turned now, and I look to him for help. He's as stumped as me. "What papers, Delia?"

"Oh, for fuck's sake. *The papers!*" she yells, slamming her fist. She rakes her chair back so suddenly it falls over.

I gasp, recoil. It's not her violence that startles me – I'm getting used to her outbursts, as much as a person can – but she *swore*. Mum never swears. Never.

Her face crumples, and she looks as if she's about to cry. God, I wish I could help her. It's frustrating for all of us, but how must she feel not being able to express herself? I move to put my arm around her. "Poor thing. Don't worry. We'll remember later."

It happens in a second. Her arm flings back and catches me across the face. "I am NOT a poor thing."

I'm so stunned, I just stand there, tasting blood, hand on my mouth. Samuel bolts across to us, grabs my shoulders and pulls me away. "It's okay, you're okay," he says. I'm not sure if he's talking to me or Mum. She looks horrified. "I'm sorry, I'm sorry," she cries, grabbing at her hair. "I don't know what's happening. I don't want this. I don't want it." Samuel leads her away to the bedroom, murmuring gentle things to her. She's sobbing, and it breaks me.

I hurry to the bathroom, wash my face, rinse blood from my mouth, try to work through what just happened. Maybe I should have let her keep going, let her calm down in her own time. How am I supposed to know the right words, the right thing to do? I run my tongue over my lower lip. There's a lump forming already.

Samuel comes up behind me, turns me around and lifts my chin. "That's going to bruise."

Oh really, Einstein, I want to say.

"Sorry," he says. "I should have seen that coming. It's been a big morning."

I twist my chin away. "Yeah. It happened so fast. No time to duck."

He pats my shoulder. "Maybe try not to patronise her so much."

I swallow. Is he blaming me? God, don't cry, not in front of Samuel. I choke my voice out. "Maybe we should think about that medication the doctor mentioned?"

He doesn't answer, just heads back to the kitchen. I follow.

He's silent as he cleans, and a spike of resentment rises in me. Is that it then? End of conversation? Wouldn't now be a good time to talk about the future? I mean tantrums are one thing, but hitting out is another. Is this the "worse" the doctor was taking about?

He pauses his washing. "I think you're right."

I look sideways at him, see the tiredness in his face, the sadness, and my anger subsides. I bite my lip. Ow! "It's the right thing," I say, hoping I'm not patronising him now.

We keep washing and drying in awkward silence. Maybe a change of subject will help. I still want to talk about my problem. The thing happening inside my t-shirt. It needs to be dealt with before the shops shut this afternoon. Before I return to school Monday. I can't handle the boys staring at me. It's too icky. I'm sure I'm the last girl in the whole school to get fitted. And I can't ask Mum, obviously. Geez, I picture her walking around the store with a bra on her head, announcing to the world that her daughter has new boobs. Maybe an exaggeration, but I've read that loss of inhibition is a common side effect of dementia, and I'm already dying inside having to ask Samuel for help.

Wait ... if I use my pocket money, I won't need to get him involved. "Samuel, could I have an advance?"

"What for?" He doesn't bother looking up, keeps scrubbing overcooked bolognaise off a saucepan – burnt cuisine is a feature lately.

"Stuff." Maybe I can slip this by him while he's distracted.

"If you need anything, you don't have to use your pocket money. Tell me what it is, and I'll get it for you."

"It's … personal stuff."

"What personal stuff?" He stops his scrubbing and turns to me. He's cranky. I've picked the wrong moment. "Be more specific. Is it for school?"

Warmth creeps into my cheeks as I purse my lips, willing the awkward words to come out.

"Girl stuff."

"Oh." Samuel scowls, then goes back to his scrubbing. "I thought we bought plenty of those with last week's shopping?"

"Not that girl stuff."

"Then what?" He turns back to me, exasperated.

I look down at my breasts, then back at him. He's still looking puzzled. I'm going to have to spell it out.

"I need … bras."

"Oh." He coughs. "Well, you don't have to use your pocket money for that. Do you… need someone to take you?"

"No!" It comes out too forcefully, and we stand, uneasy, soap dripping onto the floor from Samuel's hands. I rush to fill the silence with a sudden idea. "I'll ask Mary, Mrs Worthington, if she can drive me up to Swan Hill. She's always offering to help out."

Samuel looks relieved.

3

Escapism

Twenty minutes on a bus to Harry's place makes for a forty-five minute bike ride. No buses on Sundays. Half-a-dozen galahs forage in the scraggy bush beside the road. A few lift their fairy floss heads to investigate as I pump past on the sticky asphalt. Their beady eyes follow my motion. Nothing to see here. Just me and my sweaty efforts. Exercise is good for taking your mind off things, they say. And they may be right. Once I get to Harry's I know he'll distract me too.

I think about yelling or throwing something at the flock, for the sheer joy of seeing a cloud of pink and white take to the sky, but I leave them to their business while I keep huffing.

Up ahead is Barry Coleman's property. You can't miss it – behind the wire fence sits his annual hay sculpture. Last year it was a giant wombat, big as a barn. This year, it's a teddy bear that must be at least twelve metres high, its head, body and legs made from huge rolled bales. He's even put a happy face on it, and square ears. So cute.

When I get to Harry's drive, I stop to remove my helmet and run a hand through my sweaty hat-hair. Pushing the gate open, I try to walk-wheel my bike through without getting off it, but when I turn to shut the gate, I lose my balance. Crap! Good thing paper daisies give a soft landing. I dust my shorts and set off the few hundred metres to the homestead.

Clack, clack, clack. A twig has worked its way into the spokes of my trusty bike. The sound flashes me back to the day my dad pegged a playing card to the wheel strut of my new bicycle. I remember laughing at the rhythmic rat-a-tat-tat as I skimmed down our driveway, hair flying, sun on my face. Huh. I flick the memory away. That was another life. Besides, there's no hair-flying now. Not with Samuel. No helmet, no bike.

Harry strolls out onto the veranda. One hand holds his guitar, the other is raised to his eyes, fending off the sun's glare.

"Hi."

"Hi, yourself," I call from the bottom of the steps.

He always looks different out of school uniform. Older. Kind of dishevelled and… sexy. I blush at my own thoughts.

"You've got bedhead," I tell him.

He reaches up and ruffles his hair more. "Freedom of expression I believe it's called."

"Freedom to bullshit, you mean."

"Freedom to smack you one." He grins.

"Spell *wanker*."

"Fork you."

I rest my bike against a corroded wheelbarrow that's serving as a garden planter. It's crowded with jasmine in flower and my disturbance releases a sweet fragrance. I climb the stairs and join Harry on the porch.

"You can't talk," he says.

"What?"

"What have you got in your hair?" He reaches to pull something prickly from the side of my head. I get a whiff of his deodorant. It smells nice. Everything here smells nice.

"I fell off my bike."

"Hang on, you've got some more here."

He moves closer, and there, sticking out between us, like two camel humps, are my breasts. My new bra is making them stand to attention, and Harry's staring. And I'm staring at him. And praying that Mary, being his grandmother, hasn't let the cat out of the bag. Not that the cat isn't well and truly out, right here, right now. Harry flushes when he realises what he's doing. I'm withering with embarrassment myself, though it's somehow good to know I can have this effect on him.

"Klutz," he says, flicking away the twig he's pulled from my hair. He clears his throat, then goes over to his favourite wicker chair and sits, resting his guitar on his lap.

Awkward moment over, I climb into my favourite place: the hammock. One foot on the ground, I push off to get a good swing happening. "I'm going to ask Samuel for one of these for my birthday."

"Uh huh."

"So, what's this surprise you've got for me?" I ask.

"Patience." He strums a few chords before starting his ritual of minute twists on the knobs – machine heads, he calls them. His tongue is squished between his teeth while he concentrates on tuning his Maton. Temperature screws around with the strings. Moving from the cool of the house to the warm shade of the veranda can make a huge difference.

I relax, chewing on a long bit of dead grass I've yanked from the garden, and look up at the porch's roof, it's pretty ironwork and peeling paint. Once upon a time, it would have been pristine, but with Harry's parents often away doing their voluntourism trips to Third World countries, they have bigger priorities when they get back. Keeping their cattle alive through droughts, outweighs aesthetics. A-E-S-T-H-E-T-E … no wait … I-C-S.

It reminds me of how our family farm got run down after Dad died and how Mum lost heaps of money on it. Still, I'm glad Samuel didn't try to take it over. I can't imagine him trying to look after both Mum and the farm at the same time. Better that it was sold. And besides, if all those things never happened, I might not have moved schools and met Harry.

"So how are things going with Jessica?" I ask.

Jessica is Harry's latest. She's in his year at school, and pretty, like all the other girls he's been out with. I shouldn't be envious, because I know he's never been serious about any of them, and he's always got time to hang with me. Still, they're girls.

Harry keeps plucking. "Who?"

"Wow! Are you kidding me?"

"What are you, my mother?"

"No, but you go through girlfriends quicker than I go through Chupa Chups. What was wrong with this one?"

"Nothing. Spell inquisitorial."

"I-N-Q-U-I-S-I-T-O-R-I-A-L. Give me my Chupa Chup, and don't change the subject. Why'd you dump her?"

I wait for his answer, so I'll know not to do whatever it was Jessica did. I'm compiling a list of things he doesn't like: heavy make-up, silly laughs, airheads and neediness – girls that can't go one night without a phone call or text message from him. Which confuses me, because that's what I see when I look at all the girls he's been with.

Harry pauses his tuning, his fingers still. He looks up, annoyed. "You really wanna know?"

"Yes." I really want to know.

"She wouldn't put out."

I'm stunned. He's kidding, right? I watch his face for signs of a tell-tale smile, a giveaway smirk. But no, he starts on his strings again. I can't believe those words came out of his mouth. Not my Harry. And it shocks me to think I've never seen this side of him before. Is that why he's never made a move on me? Because I'm not the kind to "put out"? Or will he see me differently now that my body is changing?

It's ridiculous to think that a pair of lumps could change our friendship, but ... isn't that what I'm wanting? Closer attention – the stuff I think about when I'm alone. In bed. God, what happened to the simple life when we used to rough and tumble play fight and never give a thought to what body parts were touching?

"Ha! You should see your face."

"Arsehole!" I could thump him. I actually think about doing it, but that would mean fumbling out of the hammock and making an idiot of myself. And it might lead to one of those play fights that seem too weird to contemplate now. Then again, would that be so bad?

Once Harry's finished cracking himself up, he picks the same string a few times, his ear turned towards the guitar. "Nah. She kept bugging me for it."

For some reason that makes me even more angry. "So?"

"So, I couldn't help wonder who else she's been with."

"Hypocrite!"

He shrugs.

"And how many girls have you been with?" I ask.

"Not that many."

"So, there's a number on what makes a guy or a girl a... slut?"

"That's not what I meant."

"Yes, it is."

"Look, I just wasn't that into her. Anyway, it's my business who I sleep with. And for your information, I was the dump-ee, not the dump-er." Harry whacks his hand across the strings. "Done. So, here's what I've got. It's an original."

I shake my head at the speed of conversation change. I'm not ready to let it go; I've learnt more about Harry in these last five minutes than I have in the past five years. I do know enough about him, however, not to push or he'll clam up. And there's this new revelation that has my attention. I sit up and grab both sides of the hammock as it teeters.

"You wrote a song?"

So far, we've only concentrated on covers: acoustic musicians like Ed Sheeran, Colbie Caillat and Jason Mraz. Or Sarah McLachlan when Harry wants to play piano instead.

"That's so cool."

"I thought we'd use it for the school comp. Give us an extra edge."

At the mention of the competition my heart skips. I seriously wish he hadn't pushed me into signing us up. I'm an okay singer, I know that, but I'm not great in front of people. Bria Thompson, or even Keira Black, will blow me away. It's only Harry's amazing guitar that'll save us from being trodden into the mud of last place.

"Yeah, I'm still not that keen," I whine. "I mean ... not your song, I mean me. You'd be better off performing it on your own." I know what he's going to say. We've been through this before. He says his voice isn't as good as mine. I think he's in denial. His voice is fine.

"Give it a rest," he mumbles through the plastic pick he's shoved between his lips. For a second, I wonder what it would be like to have my mouth there, instead of the pick. Would his lips feel like mine? Soft and warm? Or would they be firmer, slightly rough? I turn away in case he reads my thoughts. The most he's given me is a peck on the cheek for my birthday. Maybe turning sixteen next February will be the magic number.

"They're going to wipe the floor with me."

"Get over it. We've got a month."

Nice. Still, if it means I get to spend more time with him, it's okay for now. Maybe I can feign a cold just before the competition. "Whatever. Let's hear it." I flop back and stare at the cobwebs on the ceiling. Some sort of small brown spider is working back and forth, repairing threads where a larger insect's struggle has torn webby moorings away. I wish I had that spider's resilience and confidence.

I melt as soon as Harry picks out the melancholy intro. Eyes closed, I listen as he switches to chords and sings the melody. It sounds familiar already, but new. It's not hard to imagine his deft fingers moving across the strings, gently teasing the music from his instrument. I imagine his hands strumming my skin.

Suddenly he stops and whacks a piece of paper onto my stomach. The lyrics. "Sing." I swing my legs over the side of the hammock and wait while he strums over the verse and chorus a couple more times, until I'm able to hum the whole thing. When he gets around to the opening riff again, I come in on the first verse, tentative, waiting for him to correct my phrasing. I have to admit we sound pretty good. Maybe he has a knack for choosing stuff I'm comfortable with. Stuff that suits my voice. Or maybe his confidence has rubbed off on me. Whatever it is, *maybe* we have a chance. Bring on November.

4

Predisposition

Samuel, Mum and I are all on the back porch in the dark. A cool change has kicked in after a stinker of a day. We've opened nearly every window and door, letting the breeze flush out the heat from the bedrooms and lounge. One day, Samuel promises, he'll get air conditioning put through the whole of the house, not just the kitchen and dining area.

Mum is lying on the swing chair with her feet up. She seems happier. It's taken a couple of weeks for her meds to kick in, but she seems more settled. The doctor said she might even gain more clarity, more function, temporarily. Nothing will stop the inevitable.

Samuel and I slump in deck chairs. We're sharing a basket of potato chips on a card table covered by a waratah-themed cloth that Mum cross-stitched. She's always been fussy about the niceties of serving food. If small things keep her happy, why not?

She's humming to herself. It's almost a full moon with only a few passing clouds. On nights like this, we can usually spot plenty of satellites playing hide-and-seek among the myriad of stars. I sit back in time to spot a shooting star flash across the horizon.

"Samuel? Did you see that?"

"Yep."

"Did you make a wish?"

"Yep."

"What did you wish for?"

"Well, I wished—"

"No! Don't tell me or it won't come true."

"Not going to come true anyway," he says.

The sadness in his voice is so physical it hurts.

I reach out and push Mum's swing chair, like a cradle. It's a good thing it's weighty and creaky and needs a solid effort to shove it, because like the hot house, I need to expel something heavy hanging over me. It's taken a while to figure it out. I thought I was imagining it at first, but these past few days, it's become obvious: Samuel has stopped touching Mum.

Not in the daily physical things, like getting her into the car, or making sure she steps in and out of the shower safely. No, it's the intimate things. He no longer holds her hand when they walk. Instead, he guides her, coldly and efficiently. He no longer touches her arm when he speaks to her. There's no more lifting her chin to kiss her goodbye when he leaves for work. Now it's a glancing peck on the cheek.

What's wrong with him? He's always been so close to her. Now he can hardly meet her eyes, as if looking at her will somehow spur on the monster devouring her brain. Better not risk that. Better to let it sleep, undisturbed for as long as possible. Coward. You don't stop loving someone because they're ill.

I move my chair closer to him. "Samuel. Do you think she understands?"

He grunts.

"I mean ... what's happening to her?"

"She knows."

"How do you know?"

His fist comes down hard on the card table sending the chips and his single nightly glass of beer smashing to the ground. I cringe, yanking my feet away from the shards.

"Look what you made me do!" he yells.

"Sorry."

I look at Mum. She's startled. "It's okay," I tell her, getting up to clean the mess. If I don't do it now, we'll have bull ants everywhere.

"Leave it," he says. "You'll cut yourself."

I sit, waiting for him to get up, but he doesn't. I worry about the bull ants; those terrible tiny machines with their huge pincers and stings hurt like freakin' hell. The little arseholes never seem to sleep.

Samuel sighs like a released valve on a pressure cooker. Like he's been holding his breath in forever. "Sorry. It's not your fault. I'm cranky. I chucked in my job today."

"You resigned?"

He finally gets up and squats to collect the bits of glass. "Early retirement, they call it."

He straightens and heads for the back door, his steps heavy, weary, and suddenly I'm seeing him in a new light. His job is everything to him. It's all he's ever known. Pictures from his police academy graduation, over thirty years ago, still sit on the mantelpiece above the lounge room fireplace, along with a picture of him and Mum on their wedding day, six years ago – him in police dress uniform, proud, tall, stoic, and Mum in a simple pale-yellow dress. She refused to wear a real wedding dress. It's mean to say it, but in the photo, Mum looks a little desperate, if not relieved, that someone wanted her a second time round. I'm not in any of the photos myself. I was being a little turd. I'm sad about that now.

So, Samuel is giving up his career. For Mum. If that's not true love, what is? And now the light goes on for me: he's not avoiding Mum, not repulsed by her; he's protecting himself, distancing. He's afraid of losing her. Losing who she is. But even I know avoiding stuff doesn't make it go away. Like if I don't study for a test at school, if I ignore the date coming closer and closer, it's still going to happen. I just won't be prepared for it.

I get up and fetch a bucket of water from the outside tap, bring it back and slosh it over the spilt beer. Samuel returns from the kitchen with a new glass and a whole bottle of beer. I guess he deserves it, given it's his last day at work. Commiserations and congratulations. The lemon tree will enjoy his donation later tonight. "Good for the fruit," he says. "Keeps it full and juicy."

Later, restless and tangled, I dream Mum has turned into some wild, rabid woman who tries to attack and bite us, like a zombie from The Walking Dead. One of us needs to stab her in the head. Samuel and I are both bawling our eyes out. Thankfully, I wake before we have to decide who will stick the knife in.

⚬

Samuel never watched much telly before. He preferred to read or go over police statistics for the surrounding districts. It was his thing. Now, only a couple of weeks into his retirement, he's taken to sitting with me in the evenings, after I've finished my study and Mum is tucked in bed. We don't say much. We sit, watch and keep company.

He's in his recliner with the shredded arm where Smith, Samuel's cat, used to stretch out and pad his claws into the woven fabric and pull and pull until tiny threads came loose.

Samuel would tell him off, all the while stroking his ginger bulk but doing nothing to stop the destruction. Smith's been dead over a year now. Seventeen years is a pretty good innings for a cat, I'm told. Every so often, like now, Samuel will rub the ruined fabric, but he never talks about replacing his buddy. This makes me wonder what happened to the mousing ferals we had on Dad's farm.

The toilet chime goes off, surprising us both. Samuel has installed an electric button in there so if Mum gets confused or needs help pulling her pants up, she presses and one of us will come running.

"She must have got up," Samuel says, rising.

I motion for him to stay. "I'll go." He looks wiped out now that he's looking after Mum full-time. She doesn't give him a moment's peace, always wanting him to do stuff that doesn't make sense and getting frustrated when he doesn't understand, always needing help with the smallest of tasks. I love Mum to bits, but she's become so demanding. I can't help wondering if she's playing us. My Mum would never do that, but this Mum is someone I hardly recognise any more. Even so, I think it's harder on Samuel than me. The least I can do is tag team to give him a break.

I tap on the toilet door. "Mum? It's me." I slide the door open, and the stench makes me gag. "Whoa! That's a doozy."

I stand her up, then sit her back down quickly because I nearly vomit. Something has upset her stomach. It's everywhere.

"Mum! You haven't wiped."

She gives me a blank look. I tear off a few sheets of toilet paper, then a lot more, and hold the wad out to her. She looks puzzled.

"Wipe," I say, pushing the paper at her and trying to back out of the toilet at the same time.

She nods. "Yes."

"Here." I lift her arm and try to push the paper into her hand, but she pulls back and the paper falls to the floor. She reaches for the chime button, pressing it over and over. I move her hand away, but she reaches for the chime again. Ding! Ding! Again, I tug at her hand. She settles, but her eyes are still on the button. What's going on with her? She's never done this before. "Mum, here." I try giving her some fresh paper. "Mum, you have to clean yourself."

"Yes," she says and reaches for the button. Ding! Ding! Ding!

"What is it? What do you want? Samuel? You want Samuel?"

She keeps pressing. Ding! Ding! Ding! Ding! I pull her arm away and stand in front of the button to block her access. She screams, and I panic, moving out of the way again. Then she's back at it. Ding! Ding! Ding!

"Mum! Stop it!" I slap her hand away, and she screams again. "Mum! Shush."

I'm beside myself, shaking. She falls silent, staring at the wall in front of her. I'm breathing hard, trying not to cry. Samuel comes thumping up the passage. I want to walk out and leave him to it. It's all too much, but Mum, my real mum, would die if he saw her like this.

"What's going on?"

I step out to the hall and hold my hands up. "It's okay. She's okay."

"You sure?"

"Yes. She's a just bit flustered. She's got an upset tummy. Go back to the lounge."

He looks unsure, drained and almost at his wits end, like me.

"It's okay," I reassure him. My voice doesn't sound convincing, so I say it again, stronger. "We're okay. Go."

Finally, he leaves us. I turn back to Mum and squat beside her using as gentle a voice as I can.

"Okay, Mum. I'll do it for you, alright? You don't have to worry. I'll take care of you." She says nothing, so I stand and gently lean her forwards. She doesn't resist. I reach behind her with a ridiculously large wad of toilet paper and clean her. I gag, disgust welling up inside me. Horrible, horrible disgust. My hands shake as I grasp the box of baby wipes we keep on the shelf above the toilet. I pull sheet after sheet out and soon she's as fresh as I can get her.

She lets me shower her and change her nightie before tucking her back into bed. Once she's settled, I stroke her face. "I'm sorry," I whisper, wanting to acknowledge this "loss of dignity" as Samuel would call it. But nothing registers with her. Nothing. This is how it is now. It's like she's crossed some sort of threshold.

Back in the lounge room, I sit and stare at the television, sensing Samuel watching me as I struggle to control my breathing.

"You okay, honey?" he asks.

I shake my head and crumble. I don't know if it's the term of endearment he's never used before or the gentleness in his voice, but I cry. I can't help myself. He comes over and sits beside me, wrapping me in his big arms.

"It's okay, baby."

I sob. The pain in my chest is endless. He rocks me, tight and safe. "We've got each other. We'll stick together. It'll be okay."

His breath smells like beer.

5

Chagrin

Harry helps me off the school hall stage, so I don't trip coming down like I did on the way up, klutz that I am. "See? I told you," he gloats. "We didn't bomb."

"I knew *we* wouldn't bomb," I gasp, still in shock from being called up to collect second prize, and not begrudging first place to some new guy who did an amazing drag act. Spectacular, he was, all sparkles. "It was *me* who was going to bomb. Did you see Bria Thompson's face? She couldn't believe we beat her. *I* couldn't believe we beat her."

Harry laughs. "You gotta have more faith in yourself. I keep telling you."

"You have faith in me. That's enough." I lean against the backstage wall, suddenly all shy and needing to examine the trophy in great detail.

He looks annoyed. "Come here, you nong." He grabs me into a one-armed bear hug, his other hand busy holding his guitar. The trophy pokes into our stomachs. He lets me go and stands back. "You look amazing tonight. Did I tell you that?"

I shake my head, grinning. *I did it for you,* is what I want to say, but the words get stuck.

"And if only you could hear yourself up there. You're so talented and you can't even see it. When are you going to grow up, kiddo?"

"What?" I say, the sharpness of disappointment stabbing me. Why does he always have to do that?

He leans in, lowering his mouth to my ear. OMG! He's going to kiss me. Really kiss me. Here, hidden among the dusty stage curtains and props. People cheering out there in the auditorium – not for us obviously, but it feels like it. It feels as if I'll remember this moment forever. My first kiss. Ever. With Harry. Tonight.

"When are you going to see yourself the way everyone else does?" he says.

Wait. Is he getting close because it's noisy and he thinks I can't hear him? Or because he *wants* to be close?

"And how is that?" I ask. It's excruciating. The waiting. Any second now his lips will move from my ear to my mouth. Any second now. But he falls silent. And I can't bear it. "How?" I murmur.

I know I'm fishing for compliments, but I don't care. I want him to keep talking. I want the heat of his breath on my neck. To not move. Unless it's to move closer. I want ... He shifts back a fraction, and though his eyes are so clear, I can't tell what he's thinking. What he's feeling. Conflicted?

So I do it.

I rise on my tippy toes and lift my mouth to his. A press of soft warmth, suspended, eyes closed, but the moment is over so quickly I'm crushed I didn't stay there longer, to taste him properly, to give him time to respond, to give the world time to stop turning. I open my eyes and will him: *Kiss me back.*

He's focused on my mouth, as if he's mesmerised by my quick breaths. He moves a fraction closer... then steps back. "Lauren..."

I deflate. "Yes?"

"I'm sorry."

Oh god! I've screwed up. I can see it in his eyes. What an idiot I am. I lower my head because I can't bear the rebuff that's coming.

"I've got to tell you something," he says.

And here it is. The rejection. Followed by the lame excuses.

"You're not going to like it."

I steel myself for the inevitable knock-back. The reason he can't be my boyfriend: he's known me too long, I'm too much like a sister, he's already seeing someone I don't know about. Or maybe, he simply doesn't like me *that* way?

"Look at me."

"I can't."

"Please?" He grasps my chin and turns my head. "I'm leaving."

"What?"

"I've won a scholarship. I'm going to study music in Melbourne."

It takes me a moment to absorb what he's said. "You're joking."

"No. I'm not."

"That's... that's..." A million reasons why he shouldn't go are circling my brain, but none make it to my lips, because they're all selfish. I'm dizzy, struggling to process...

"Are you okay?" he says.

"When?"

"After graduation. Just before Christmas. Mum and Dad are selling the farm. They got an amazing deal, much more than they expected. They're going travelling again. Overseas. And I'm moving to Melbourne. It's all happened so quickly. They were made an offer. I got the acceptance—"

"No, I mean when did you know about this?"

He hesitates. "Not long. I didn't tell you because I didn't want to upset you before—"

"The competition? Our exams next week? Thanks. That's great."

"It's not immediate. I'm going to see out the year."

"A few weeks. Not even Christmas. Awesome."

"That's why I can't... why we shouldn't..."

"Yep, yep." I wave him off. "You don't have to explain. I'm happy for you. Really."

Everything is crashing in around me. My face is on fire. I want to push him away because it hurts so much, but it's not his fault. It's mine. I waited too long. "It's fine. Totes. Here, take this. It's yours." I shove the trophy at him.

I need to put space between us. Get some air. I fumble my way through the rows of curtains in search of the rear stage door. There's a big sign across it that says "Do Not Open". Alarmed Door'. I don't care. I barge through it, and the clanging starts immediately. I turn and shove the door closed behind me. The noise stops.

In the car park, the night air still holds the heat of the day, and it hits me hard after the air conditioning of the theatre. Where to go? Anywhere. I walk between the cars, but my heels – which I wore for Harry, thinking he might like me better if I looked like all the other pretty girls he's dated – get caught and sink in the dead-grass parking lot. I tear them off and continue in my bare feet.

"Well done," I mutter. "Epic fail." I finally find a stump to sit on, not caring if the raw bark edges tear my dress – the filmy one I've saved up all my pocket money for, because I thought he'd like me to look more girly.

God. What a drama queen. I left him there, guitar in one hand, stupid trophy in the other, and stormed off like the kid he keeps saying I am. Maybe he's right. My face burns so much I can't tell if it's my mortification or the heat.

Take five, I tell myself. It's not the end of the world. He's not dying. He's just leaving. To study. I pause to recall and analyse each of his words: amazing, talented. Not words you say to someone you love. The words that count the most came after I'd kissed him: "*That's why I can't*" and "*Why we shouldn't*". Not *I really like you but...* or *I think you got the wrong idea*. He's leaving. It's not a rejection. It's a relocation. And now there's a little bud of hope that survives.

I'm leaning against the Carters' car, waiting to live down my embarrassment, as Harry and his family approach. I figure he's told them I'd run off, so there's no avoiding it – they've given me a lift to the concert. Thank god I didn't resort to crying. Nothing like a mascara-streaked face to give away a drama queen. A kid.

"Ah, Lauren," says Mr Carter. "Harry said you'd probably be waiting here. Congratulations. What an exciting win."

I glance at Harry, grateful he hasn't told them after all. "Yeah. Thanks."

We sit in the back seat, shoulder to shoulder, knee to knee, his little sister taking up half the space with her booster seat. Every press of our bodies, the warmth of our skin, reminds me of our earlier closeness.

"Hey," he whispers. "Talk to me."

I so want to lean into him, tuck my head into his shoulder, to breathe in his scent, feel the vibration of his voice through his chest. Instead, I stare at the invisible landscape outside the window.

"Spell *chagrin*," he says.

He's humiliated? He doesn't know what the word means. I shake my head, afraid that whatever he has to say will be salt in my wounds. He touches my arm, and I let him. Pulling away would be more childishness.

"I'm sorry I didn't tell you. I really didn't think I'd get the scholarship. I still can't believe it."

I nod.

"Speak to me, will you?"

I want to. So much. I'm afraid if I do, I'll be a blubbering mess, and then I'll look more of an idiot than I already feel. I just can't imagine him not being here. He's been in my life since forever. And I died a little more each time he broke up with another girlfriend and didn't see me. I was right there all the time. Why didn't he *see* me? Now my heart is hanging out, raw and bleeding.

I swallow, trying to ease the lump in my throat. "It's okay," I manage.

"No, it's not."

"I'm happy for you," I mumble.

"No, you're not."

"No." Not yet.

He goes quiet, and we sit while his parents chat in the front, the occasional headlights of passing cars flashing over our picture of unhappiness in the back seat. His little sister is blissfully asleep. Harry takes my hand. When I try to pull away, he holds firm. I relent, but I still can't look at him.

6

Dissimulation

Late morning, the chooks look as though they're suffering from the heat, so after I empty the kitchen scraps into their pen, I give them a spray with the hose. They squawk and flap, feathers sprinkling water droplets that catch the sunlight. Pretty.

"Are you okay there?" I ask Mum.

She's resting on the porch swing, in the shade. "Yes, love."

I head back inside to continue my exam studies. If I can just get by this next week, I'll be done, but it only takes Mum a couple of minutes to start calling. I get up from the kitchen table and peer through the back door screen. She's barefoot on the grass, staring at the wet washing hanging heavy on the clothesline. She lowers her gaze to the concrete base where a scuffed ice cream container sufficing as a peg basket sits. I shrink back as she turns and glances at the house. Can she see me watching behind the flyscreen? We only hung the washing a few minutes ago, and now she wants to take it down again.

"Ah, Mum," I whisper. "Why can't you stay where I left you with your magazines?" It's too freakin' hot to be chasing after her, and I really, really need to study. I suppose I'm a bit cranky at her, to be honest – she snapped on my bedroom light around four this morning and told me I was lazy for sleeping in so late. I was furious from the fright and from being so freakin' tired. Sigh.

She calls again.

I swing the screen door open. "Mum, come inside. Let's have some tea."

She turns mechanically; her body has stiffened the past week. I wonder if we need to get her meds increased. "Samuel?" she calls. What's going through her mind? Is she torn between doing her wifely duties with the washing or obeying me, a daughter she used to give the orders to? Or is there something completely off the planet going on? Like ... is the washing talking to her?

"Come on, Mum. Samuel will be back from shopping soon. Then we'll have some lunch." The magic word "lunch" doesn't work. Usually food is like a bone to a dog for her, but today maybe the lure of whispering washing is too great. She stays put. At least she's wearing a hat, so the sun won't scorch her. I give up and go back inside to put the kettle on – in case she manages to get her head around a cup of tea.

I'm finally getting into my biology textbook, reading how Louis Pasteur disproved that fermentation was due to "spontaneous generation", when our front gate creaks. "Faaarrrk!" I thump my fist on the table. How did she get around to the front of the house so quickly? Screw Louis and his spontaneous generation. If I don't get five minutes' peace, *I'm* going to spontaneously combust.

I hurry to the lounge room and look through the lace curtains. It's not Mum, it's Mary. She's probably bringing the latest newsletter, even if Mum can't sit still a moment to read it anymore. Crap. Samuel says I'm not allowed to let anyone in the house now, which makes things rude and awkward because Mary has been so helpful and kind to us with pots of casseroles and soups, or fresh fruit and veg from her garden. Just because Mary suggested it might be time to think about a hospice for Mum, Samuel cracked it.

"But why?" I argued. "It can't be good for Mum to be cut off from everyone."

"I've had enough. It's none of their business."

"But Mary's known Mum since forever. She's her best friend."

"This is my house and my rules. We can manage."

Arsehole.

Mary is picking her way through the rockery. She has a tea towel-covered basket balancing on her arm, and she looks determined. How am I going to deflect her? I don't have Samuel's bulk to stand in the doorway and intimidate people. It's ridiculous trying to hide Mum, anyway. Her friends all know what's was going on. Everyone does.

The doorbell chimes. Mary stands firm in her pristine bowls uniform. She smiles, big and cheery.

"Hello, Lauren. We had our monthly cake stall this morning. It's not the same without your mum's apple crumble, but I've brought morning tea."

I bite my lip. "Samuel isn't here at the moment." I'm sure I don't need to explain what I mean.

"Correct. I saw his jeep's not in the drive. That's okay," she says, pushing past me. "Us girls can manage without."

She places her basket on the kitchen table and lifts out a plate of scones. "Oh, there you are, Delia. Good to see you."

Mum has shuffled in from outside, the peg bucket in her hands. I'm glad I insisted on her wearing jeans and a cotton shirt today instead of her dressing gown – it gets so grubby – but getting it off her is like trying to twist a tight lid off a jar when you have greasy fingers. This morning I distracted her with the promise of her favourite ice cream, which she's since forgotten. Now, she fixes her eyes on the scones.

"Come sit," says Mary. "We've all been worried about you." She moves to give Mum a kiss. "Where are your shoes?"

Mum looks down, puzzled.

"We were having a sit on the grass out back," I rush. "A bit of sun. I'll get her slippers." I realise how ridiculous I sound. No-one sits out in the midday sun if they value their lives: Mallee bloom is one thing, but skin cancer is rife out here.

Mum doesn't challenge my explanation. She's still focused on the scones.

"Sit down. Help yourself," Mary says, pulling out a chair for Mum. "I've got jam and cream in here too. Make us a cuppa will you, Lauren? And we'll need some knives and spoons too."

I grab the peg bucket from Mum and decide to forgo her slippers. Instead, I clear my study books from the table.

Mum sits. "Thank you, Mary. It's been a while since I cooked scones. I have to be careful now. Burns, you know. How are the bowls girls? I miss them."

I'm gob-smacked at Mum's clarity.

The kettle is still hot, so I fill the teapot, fetch cups, plates and cutlery and take a seat next to Mum. "Here you go," I say, passing Mum a spoon so she won't attack the cream with her fingers. She accepts it, allowing me a touch of hope this might not go so badly. She reaches for a scone and manages to spread jam on it without mashing it into a bready mess. Mary asks her how she is.

"Oh, Mary!" Mum says, looking surprised. "How are you, Mary?"

"Well, thanks. And you've been to the doctor a while ago, I hear?"

"Yes, the doctor," Mum says through a mouthful of scone, cream oozing out the side of her mouth.

"And is everything okay?"

"Yes." She nods. "Still going mad. All good."

I look at Mary and choke back a laugh. Mary chuckles too. If Mum stays lucid, maybe, just maybe, Mary will have her tea and scoot before Samuel gets back. It's a shame, though. Having a friend to talk to seems to be keeping Mum's mind focused. Maybe it could even slow her deterioration. God, life is so complicated. Better to toe the line, though. Besides, as much as I'm pissed at Samuel, I kind of agree that Mum should be allowed a "dignified degradation" as he calls it, without people gawking at her. Then again, Mary isn't just "people".

"Lauren?"

I look up.

Mary nods at my plate. "You're not eating?"

"Not really hungry, thanks. Samuel will be back soon, and we'll have lunch."

"Got to get the washing in," Mum says, pushing her chair back.

I sigh. I've been too hopeful. "No, Mum. It's still wet." I get up to ease her back into her seat.

She looks at me angrily. "Don't be stupid. It's been out since yesterday. It'll be fried to a crisp." She pushes her chair back further.

"Mum, we only put it out a few minutes ago."

"Let go of me!" she yells.

And I do, because while I can handle her vagueness, I can't handle her anger, her aggression towards me. It hurts, feels personal, as much as Samuel keeps telling me it's not. As she heads out the back door, I shrug at Mary and sit again. "What can you do?"

She reaches over and puts her hand on mine. "It's okay."

I hate the tears that suddenly well. I hate the impulse to rush over, wrap my arms around her pudgy waist and bury my face in her motherliness.

Her voice is soft, knowing. "Lauren, if you ever need someone—"

"Yes!" declares Mum, trundling back in with a ragged-looking bunch of weeds in her hand. She dumps them on the table, soil and all, then picks up her abandoned scone. Mary and I both watch as she takes a huge bite, spilling jam down the front of her shirt.

"Delia," Mary says. "You're supposed to eat it, not wear it." She takes a napkin from her basket and holds it out to Mum.

I have to check myself from automatically taking it and wiping Mum's chin. The napkin hangs from Mary's hand as we all stare and wait. Finally, Mum clicks and registers its purpose.

"That good, are they?" I ask.

"Yes!" she says, mid-wipe.

"Well, okay," I relent. "I guess I'll have some then. Just a half. I don't want to ruin Samuel's lunch." I'm hoping the mention of Samuel again will sink in, and maybe if I have a scone, Mary will be happy and leave us alone before he gets back.

As I reach over to the plate, Mum smacks down her spoon and announces, "You know we had a brown snake in the house yesterday?"

Mary nearly chokes, mid-swallow. She coughs up soggy scone bits into a hastily grabbed napkin. "What?"

"A snake. Brown one. It came crawling out of the bedroom and into the kitchen. Went behind the cabinet there. The snake catcher couldn't find it."

Mary blanches, looking over her shoulder to the hallway.

It's true. We did have a snake, and it freaked us all out, but I feel sorry for Mary, so I try to reassure her.

"It's gone. We left the door open for a while. The snake guy said he was pretty sure it would have gone outside."

Mary looks behind her. "This cabinet?"

"Yep," I say. "Probably gone, though." It's now I realise the opportunity Mum's given me. "*Probably*."

Mary pushes her chair back and stands. "I don't know whether to believe you or not," she says.

"It's true, isn't it, Mum?" I hold my breath, fairly sure I can get another "yes' out of her.

"Yes."

Thank you. I can't believe Mum has saved us.

Mary picks up her purse and basket. "Okay, I get the message." She sounds resigned. My relief turns to pity. I shrug and smile a "sorry', hoping she'll pick up on it. At the door, she turns. "Remember what I said. You and Harry are in the middle of exams. You shouldn't be under this stress. If it gets too much—"

"I will. Thanks. And if you could not say anything ... you know ... Samuel."

She nods and makes a motion of turning a lock over her lips.

I watch through the lounge room curtains until she shuts the front gate and disappears from view. When I turn back, Mum is busy stacking three scones on top of each other using the jam and cream as mortar. Does she know what she's just done? Sending Mary packing like that? I sit again, picking up my unfinished scone. Should I tell Samuel I made them, or come clean? I'm sure he'll know I'm lying. I'm crap at it. Tough. What happens, happens. I can't control the world.

7

Unrequited

Trish, the café owner, is standing on a chair, re-pinning tinsel that's fallen down – ten days until Christmas. I'm just about to offer my help, when my vision is obscured by a pair of hands. No prizes for guessing who's sneaked up behind me.

"Guess who?" he says anyway.

"Michael Jackson?"

Harry lets go and flops into the chair opposite. "Because I'm such a smooth criminal?"

"No. Because you're about to Beat It."

"Ha." He plonks a terribly wrapped, odd-shaped present on the café table. I pick it up and shake it. It doesn't rattle. "I think I'm the one who's supposed to give you a present."

He shrugs. "Something to remember me by."

And there's the lump in my throat I've been fighting all week, knowing this day was coming. "Thanks," I choke out.

"Hey, hey, save that for tomorrow when I'm gone. You don't get to be a sook today. Today is about fun. All day. *Fun.* You hear me?"

Trish comes over to take our orders. She's heard Harry is leaving. Everybody knows everything in this town. "Guess we'll have to cut down on stocking Chupa Chups, hey?" she says.

Harry laughs. "Either that or Lauren can post me my winnings."

"Fat chance," I say. "I'll have a raspberry shake and a cheeseburger. And he'll have a fried peanut butter and banana sandwich."

Harry frowns. "Ewww. She's joking. I'll have the same, thanks." Trish leaves us and Harry looks at me, puzzled. "Peanut butter and banana?"

"Think about it."

"Elvis?"

"Yep."

"I still don't get it."

"You will."

He mulls it over for a minute, then a light goes on. "Cos I'm about to *leave the building*." He smirks. "Your music taste is crap. You've got to stop listening to Samuel's records."

"I don't have a freakin' choice. He hogs the sound system, day and night. He says retro is in."

"That's not retro, that's one foot in the grave."

"Yet, you still know it."

"Touché. Why don't you ask him for an iPhone for Christmas, so you can download your own music?"

"Maybe."

"Are you still pissed at me?"

"I'll always be pissed at you."

"At least open your present."

I tear into the package. "It's not some dumbass snow globe is it?"

There's layer after layer of paper. He's screwed up bits of paper and cardboard and tucked them inside the wrapping to disguise the size and shape of the present. The pile of discarded, torn paper grows until I'm left with a small square object in what feels like the last piece of wrapping. For a millisecond I picture a ring box. But that's idiotic. It turns out to be a teeny-weeny dictionary. I smile as I flip it open to a page of teeny-weeny writing.

"It's cute."

"There's an inscription," he says. "In the front."

I turn the pages back until I find it: *You're the flip side.* "What does it mean?"

"It's a reference to one of my favourite lyrics. It reminds me of you. Google it tomorrow when I'm gone."

When I'm gone. I swallow, determined not to cry. I hold up the dictionary. "Thanks. But how's that going to work, you nong? Texting words to each other?"

"Ever heard of a phone call?"

"It's not the same. It's our bus game. Anyway, you'll just cheat and look up the words."

He narrows his eyes and points a finger at me. "Only another cheat would think of that."

Our burgers are good and messy. When we're finished, Harry drives us up to Swan Hill to see a movie – his dad has let him borrow the car for one night. The movie is some crime, action, spy, mystery thing and halfway through a tense scene, where the hero is about to be shot in the guts, Harry grabs my hand. I jump.

"Sorry," he whispers, chuckling.

"No, you're not."

I expect him to let go. He doesn't. I can't concentrate with the heat of his touch, the little squeezes now and then, and the furtive looks we give each other.

"You're not watching," he whispers.

"Neither are you."

"Wanna ditch it?"

"Yeah."

We head towards a park alongside the Murray River, and we walk, still holding hands, as if it's perfectly natural. I'm blissed out being with him but gutted too; this is as close as we'll ever be. My best friend is leaving. Three years of uni seems like a lifetime. Even if I were to follow him to the city once I've finish my VCE, a lot can happen in a year. He's sure to find someone else by then. He's too hot not to. Some lucky city girl is gonna have my guy.

We stop and watch a bunch of gulls circling the light above a riverside building. Their lonely calls carry in the quiet. Harry is humming something.

"What's that?" I ask.

"Smile."

"Huh?"

"Google will tell you tomorrow."

"Spell *irksome*."

"Spell *patience*."

He pulls my hand and we keep walking through the tepid evening. Dark and light, light and dark, under the streetlamps. I'm listening to him hum, trying to make out the melody. It's familiar, but I can't place it. He's still humming when we find a bench and sit to look out over the river. The park lights are stars sprinkled on the water.

"Why does it remind you of me?" I ask at last.

"Because ... it says everything about you."

I blink, warmth filling me. "It does?"

"Yeah. It's you and you don't even know it."

He leans in then and kisses me. Short and soft. He puts his arm around me and pulls me to his side. I rest my head on his shoulder the way I've always wanted to. He still smells nice. His voice rumbles low. "I'm gonna miss you, buddy."

Buddy. "Me too."

There are no more kisses and tomorrow there will be no more Harry.

<hr>

It's midnight, and I can't sleep. Can't wait any more. I get out of bed, turn my laptop on and type "You're the flip side". A bunch of urban dictionary definitions come up. Is he calling me a vinyl record? What does that even mean? No wait, he said something about a lyric. I trawl back through our conversation. Then it clicks. I add the word "smile" to my search. It takes only seconds for the results to come up. It's a song by Uncle Kracker. The lyrics are beautiful: he sings about how lucky he is to have this girl in his life, how she makes him smile and sends away the rain. She's a flower. She makes him dizzy. Google just broke my heart.

<hr>

Mum's meds have stopped working. She's taken to watching for the postman, convinced he's stealing our mail instead of delivering it. She waits by the front window like a guard dog, twitching at the curtain and screeching to Samuel when she sees the guy's motorbike stop at our gate. It's terrifying.

8

Stupefaction

Geez, hurry up autumn. This late-February heat is doing nothing for my mood at having spent a month of the new school year without Harry. And now, to add to my torment, I've walked in to Billy Joel and Samuel wailing about a piano sounding like a carnival. I dump my bag and meander through to the kitchen. Samuel grabs my arms and swings me around. He's drunk!

"Look! Look!" he says, pointing to the dining table. I grin, distracted from his state. He's remembered. There's a cake from the bakery – chocolate with cream and berries between the layers and white chocolate shavings on top. He's even gone to the trouble of ordering a little plaque with "Happy 16th Birthday Laurie". Never mind the spelling.

I'm genuinely impressed. I thought everyone had forgotten. I couldn't expect Mum to remember, but no present, no card, not even a text from Harry. Nothing. Too busy with uni, I expect. It hurts to have to reason away his lack of thought. And I'm not one of those people who tells Facebook my birth date, so no happy birthdays from fake friends either.

But here, look at this delicious dessert. "Thanks, Samuel," I gush, giving him a kiss on the cheek. Strange how once that would have felt awkward with our former arms-length relationship, but lately things have shifted, and it feels okay now. It feels right. I go over and give Mum a kiss too, but she's too busy ogling the chocolate mountain in front of her.

"It looks great," I say, heading to the sink to start the vegetables for dinner.

"Leave it," Samuel says, dragging me back to the table. "Let's go crazy and have cake for dinner." He's all red-faced and smiles. I've never seen him like this. I like it.

Samuel and I eat two slices each and stall on the third, while Mum has been busy making a mound of brown and red mush on her plate and spooning it up with the help of her fingers. Samuel gives a satisfied sigh and leans his arm over the back of the chair beside him. I go to the bathroom and bring back a damp face washer for Mum, and as I start to wipe her sticky fingers, I reflect how once upon a time she would have been cleaning my baby fingers.

Samuel jumps to his feet and grabs the washer from me. "Not tonight."

I blink. Not sure I understand.

"Put the kettle on," he says. "I'll take care of Mum."

"You sure?" I'm reluctant to hand Mum over to him in his drunkenness, but he seems to have sobered a bit with the sugary food.

"Birthday," he says, and grins.

I clean the few dishes, then make Samuel some tea, and a Milo for me. I should be revising for my maths test tomorrow, but hell, I know my stuff, and it's my birthday.

I wait in the lounge room, hearing the toilet flush, the tap running, the electric toothbrush, then Samuel and Mum's voices murmuring in the bedroom as he puts her to bed with the little telly he's bought for her bedside table.

Samuel sinks onto the couch beside me. He's given up his recliner since the "night of shit". Sometimes he just sits and stares at the telly, lost in his thoughts and a couple of beers. Other nights he clutches my hand, the way he clutched Mum's hand at the doctor's that day we went to hear her diagnosis. I like the nights when he doesn't clutch, but rather holds my hand gently and pats it now and then. It's way different to how Harry held my hand. It's as though he's comforting me. Or maybe himself. Whatever, I treasure the closeness, the softening of him. I think this is what real dads are like. It's nice.

It's still early, a little after seven. The front door is open to let in the evening breeze, and a mass of cockies are squawking from their regular perch – the power lines across the street. We're watching a current affairs program, something about the government ripping off farmers by selling water rights to foreign companies, when Samuel lets out a weird noise, as if he's strangling. At first it startles me. Is he ill? Then I realise what's happening, and it frightens the hell out of me because, in all the time we've been living together, all eight years, I've never seen Samuel cry.

The pain on his crumpled face is unbearable, and I fight not to cry myself. I know what it's about. I know. I just don't know what kicked it off. There's been no screaming or fuss from Mum. It must be everything. All piled on top of him. And the alcohol. He's broken at last. It's my turn to comfort him. I try to put my arm around his bulky shoulders as they shudder. He burps, the smell a strange combination: sweetness of cake and sourness of second-hand beer. He turns to me, burying his sobs in my shoulder and putting his hand around my waist. I hug him tight.

Eventually he calms and rests his head back against the sofa, eyes closed. He sniffs and swallows the gunk in his throat. "Sorry," he mumbles.

"It's okay. Happens to the best of us."

He laughs, then hiccups. "Been coming for a long time."

"Yep."

"Didn't see it coming today. Sorry, I'm ruining your birthday."

"You're not. It's okay. Maybe go easy on the beer for a while though."

"You're a wise girl."

It's now that I'm conscious of his hand still on my thigh. Awkward. But I don't want to draw attention to it; he might feel embarrassed or, worse, rejected. I wait. He'll realise soon enough and remove it himself.

A reality home renovation show is starting. Samuel hates reality TV. Maybe he'll come to and reach for the remote. No luck. I turn to look at him. He's asleep. How does he do that? It's like somebody's hit an off button. I shift sideways and mercifully his hand slides off me. I'm not sure whether to go to bed and leave him here or shake him awake to make him go to bed himself. When in doubt: tea. I head to the kitchen.

It's strange being the only one in the house who's awake. Samuel is always the last to go to bed, checking the doors, turning lights off, turning the dishwasher on to chug quietly into the night. He's always the first up too. I glance around the kitchen, looking at stuff that's so familiar I've always taken it for granted: the Nescafé cups Mum won through a magazine competition, the Royal Dansk butter cookie tin someone gave us for Christmas a few years back, now full of Samuel's extra strong peppermint lollies. And the stuff that's alien because I never noticed it creep into the everyday clutter: an odd-shaped jug that once held some sort of orange liqueur, a row of bulldog clips stuck to the rim of the fruit bowl. It strikes me how we live in the same rooms every day yet never notice the gradual changes happening, accumulating – like Mum's dementia.

I place Samuel's tea on the coffee table and sit next to him while I sip another Milo. His face shows no signs of stirring. Ruddy jowls hang under his five o'clock shadow – something else I hadn't noticed before. I look for other signs of his ageing: his developing paunch, salt and pepper eyebrows (too long), spidery veins on his cheeks. Is this because of how we live now? The heaviness of it? Is it ageing me too?

Other girls my age are wearing make-up, kissing boys, piling in older brother's cars to see a rock band in another town. Having fun. Being normal. Not me. Harry was the closest I ever came to having a boyfriend. Now he's gone, and all I have left is the teeny-tiny dictionary he gave me. And I haven't made any new friends because everyone's got their cliquey groups from previous years. No-one could ever fill Harry's shoes anyway. What's the point of trying?

"Do you have a boyfriend?" Samuel asks so suddenly I jolt, spilling a few drops of my Milo. How weird he wakes and asks that right at this moment.

"Not really," I mumble, brushing my skirt.

"What's that?" He brings his head forwards and looks at me with bleary eyes.

"No."

"Why not?"

I shrug. "There was someone. But he's gone."

"Harry? You liked him?"

Here comes the rising flush in my cheeks. Why can't Samuel stick to our normal conversation: Have you done your homework? Have you watered the garden? Have you changed Mum's wee pads?

Well, he doesn't call them *wee pads*. But *that* is our usual conversation, not embarrassing boy talk. Is he going to tell me all about sex now?

"Yeah."

"Huh. Has Mum talked to you about boys?"

Oh god. *Please.* I nod, even though it isn't true. She's been sick for so long, and somehow we never got around to it. The internet has been my theoretical teacher. The prac is yet to come.

"What's that?"

"Yeah. Yes, she has."

"Good."

He rises and goes to the kitchen. A chicky babe on the renovation show is complaining about the price of a lampshade, while Samuel's tea sits cold and milky. Chicky. Sigh. Mum used to call me that when she was in a good mood.

Samuel returns with two stubbies of Carlton Draught. "Want one?" he offers.

I shake my head.

"I won't tell anyone," he says, holding it out to me.

I refuse again so he puts the spare on the table, then sinks back, twisting his bottle cap. The television chick is looking pleased with herself. She got a discount on the lampshade.

We sit like that for a while, Samuel sipping and staring, staring and sipping, the light fading outside and the cockies mustering into a nearby gum for the night. My eyes are drooping when Samuel suddenly slaps my knee. "Bunch of crap," he says, pointing to the telly. Chicky babe is standing, hands on hips, looking at a security camera screen she's had installed. It gives a view of a front porch and driveway.

"Bloody city folk. Scared in their own homes," he says, his hand resting on my thigh again.

———◆———

Six empty stubbies sit at Samuel's feet, and one lies on its side, a drizzle of beer leaving a dark stain on the carpet. Samuel's head is flopped against the back of the couch again, his mouth slack, on the verge of snoring. He's opened his shirt, complaining it was too tight. Grey hairs curl over the top of his singlet. Mum's brass clock on the mantel begins its eleven o'clock chime, its pendulum swinging lazily back and forth with each ping. The digital clock at the other end of the mantel clicks over as well. Samuel dug the black plastic thing out of his garage the day after he was late to a council meeting – once – because the brass clock had seized. Now red LEDs angle towards the brass clock, as if in competition, glaring all night long. It's a good thing Mum's ceramic vase sits between them or they'd have a punch up.

Samuel snorts awake.

"I'm going to bed," I say. "You should too." I don't know why I've stayed up this late already, being a school night. I guess I didn't want to leave Samuel alone in his state.

"Uh?" He looks surprised, as if he's forgotten I was there. Or maybe he's wondering why he's in the lounge room and not in bed himself. His cold tea is still on the coffee table. I stand and collect it with my own empty cup. As I do, he grips my wrist and pulls me back. I stumble, spilling tea over my skirt and Samuel's legs. I fall heavily onto the couch beside him, spilling more tea. He jumps as if he's been scalded.

"Sorry," he slurs.

"It's okay," I say, trying to hold what's left of the tea upright.

He stands and helps me to my feet – him wobbly in his drunkenness and me in my tiredness. "You're a good girl, Lauren."

I give a half smile. "Uh huh."

"Don't know what I'd do without you."

He grabs either side of my face and squeezes. Probably harder than he means to. "You're a good girl," he repeats. I try to pull away, embarrassed by the intimacy, but both my hands are full. "You look so…" Something passes over his face. Something strange I don't understand, or like.

"Samuel."

"You look so… like your mum," he drawls. "When she was young. I loved her then, you know. Bastard beat me to her."

"Samuel, you're hurting me."

He lets go and shoves his hands in his pockets. "Sorry. Yeah. Bedtime." He steps back and lets me pass. I scurry to the kitchen, then to the bathroom.

As I brush my teeth, I can't help checking my reflection. Of course, I look like Mum. Who else would I look like? Same heart-shaped face; dark eyes; small, round nose, though mine is a touch pointier. We share the same dimpled chin, but that's where the similarities end because she's tall, slender, like a 1950s magazine model and everything looks good on her. I got the short straw. And now her hair has been cut short to keep things low maintenance and to stop her hacking at it herself, while mine still falls past my shoulders.

Samuel's heaviness shuffles past the bathroom door, and the hydraulic thingy on the rear screen door hisses. It's a new sound to the household; Mum can't handle loud noises now. Samuel will be off to visit the lemon tree out back.

I ease open the bathroom door and sneak off to my room.

At first, I think it's the peppercorn tree groaning outside my window that's woken me. The night has turned all hot and blustery, the kind where the wind picks up anything not tied down, and dirt deposits into every crevice. I roll over and check my phone. It's nearly four o'clock. I push my covers off, restless, sweaty, headachy. Maybe I'm coming down with something? Crap. My maths test is today. No way am I going to be able to concentrate. That's a big fat "F"coming right up. Water. I need water.

No point tiptoeing; there isn't a pattern to the creaks in the hallway floorboards. One week this side squeaks, the next the other. It doesn't matter anyhow as Samuel and Mum's bedroom is at the other end of the house, past the kitchen. And besides, Samuel is a log once he hits his pillow, one that sounds as if it's being sawed. Add the alcohol he's drunk tonight, and I bet a Mack truck wouldn't wake him.

I'm wrong. As I pass the lounge room I freeze. A bulky shape looms in the middle of the room. "Samuel?" I whisper. "Are you still up?" The lights are out, and the digital clock is bathing the room in a red flashing glow. 16:01. The power must have gone out during the night with the storm.

Samuel murmurs something I can't make out.

"Did you fall asleep on the couch?" I ask.

I reach for the light switch and flip it on. Stunned, wide-eyed and open-mouthed, it takes me a few seconds before I gain the sense to spin around and flick the light back off. It's too late. I've already seen that his pants are down around his ankles and ...

I stand with my back to him, trying to equate what I've seen to something else. Maybe he's holding something in front of him, the remote control. Or maybe his belt is somehow folded and sticking out in front of him. It's no use. I've never seen a real penis before, only pictures, but I instinctively know what I saw. What do I do? Pretend nothing's happened? There's movement behind me, the rustle of clothing. He's probably dressing himself, as embarrassed as I am.

I move to go back to my room, but he calls to me. "Don't go."

I pause, my back to him. "Samuel, why aren't you in bed?"

"Lonely." His voice is ragged, as though he's been crying again. "She doesn't want me there. It frightens her. She thinks I'm a stranger."

My heart breaks for him, but my head tells me to leave. I turn, my eyes adjusting to the dark again. He's sobbing, like before. What do I do? I can't leave him here in this state. I reach for his arm.

"Come on, lie on the couch. I'll get you some blankets."

He leans on me, one arm around my shoulders as I try to guide him. He stumbles. I can't support his weight; I tumble with him. The coffee table turns over, empty beer bottles clink and scatter around us. Winded, I lie there with his bulk pressing me to the floor, a bottle digging into my thigh.

I try to shove him, but he grabs my hand and pins it. His mouth is hot and horrible, all over on my face. I try to scream. No breath.

"Samuel! No! Get off me."

◆

When it's over, and my shower hasn't been able to wash and scrub away the revulsion, I crawl into bed and scrunch into a tiny ball. My stomach clenches with nausea. I cover my ears, trying to forget the sounds of my crying and his panting and grunting. The tree outside my window is still groaning.

9

Abnegation

I wake to a wattlebird screeching. Those first few seconds, my head is quiet and dull. Then it all comes flooding back. I pull the doona over my head. I don't know how to face the day. How to face Samuel. Mum. Who do I tell? *Do* I tell? Maybe I'll pretend nothing's happened, go about business as usual. Samuel was drunk. He probably won't even remember. But I do. What should I do? The question goes round and round with no answer.

I want another shower. I still feel dirty. But I don't want to move. Moving means facing it. And then the doubt creeps in. Was it my fault? I'd let him sit close, hold my hand, hold me. *It's never the victim's fault.* There's been so much chatter on the news and online lately about victim blaming. And there, in a split second, I've become something that never, ever occurred to me: a victim. I'm not me anymore. Where did I go? Crazy, I've gone crazy.

I move through the house, numb with lack of sleep, edgy with wariness. Their bedroom door is open, but neither Samuel nor Mum is up. Something's not right. No snoring. I'm guessing Samuel is dead to the world after his drinking, and Mum's still dopey from her sleeping pills. I slip into the bathroom and lock the door.

I desperately want to shower again, to scrub away the memory of him, but the thought of being naked, with Samuel nearby, even in drunken sleep, even with the bathroom door locked...

How did I manage last night?

I listen, straining to hear for any movement. I take my top off for a quick wash with a face cloth. I stop and listen again, towel pressed tightly to my chest, then hurry with the rest of my wash. I can't look in the mirror; I don't want to see this other self I've become. I know I'll start crying, and that can't happen. I have to push everything down, keep it tight and knotted, so I don't fall apart.

It's too early, but I leave the house anyway, keeping the snick of the front door as quiet as I can. I straighten my uniform and pat down my hair as I walk up the drive, then open the gate only a fraction, so it doesn't creak too much. The footpaths are swept with soil from last night's wind. Shifting piles of red dirt sit in the cracks and gutters. Branches and leaves coat the roads.

I head to the café, where Trish tells me I've missed the early bus. My regular one is in another twenty-five minutes. I order a hot chocolate and sip while I stare at my maths book. Trish brings me a blueberry muffin. "It's yesterday's," she says. "Free." Can she tell? Am I a walking, flashing sign that reads "Molested"?

I nod, unable to return her smile.

She goes back to the counter but keeps glancing at me. *Can* she tell? Country folk always seem to know each other's business. It's like the osmosis we learnt about in biology class. Only it's not water or gas particles, it's gossip, seeping from one person to the next, household to household. Not today. No way. Not talking is the first step to forgetting.

When the bus is nearly due, I grab some minty gum and head out. I concentrate on unwrapping the gum, the crackling plastic helping me to focus, to keep my mind busy. The bus stop is only a five-minute walk: past the pub that I'm too young to work at, past the butcher's with prices too high because of drought, past the chemist, and the hairdresser that operates only on Mondays and Thursdays. I look at the window dressings and read all the sale signs and community notices, so I don't have time to think.

Bill doesn't notice my messed-up state as I climb the bus steps. Not that he notices much usually. He hardly looks at who's getting on or off, his droopy seen-too-much-bullshit eyes always focused on the road ahead. He closes the door, reaches for the gear stick, flicks a look in the side mirror, then pulls out. Routine can be a drug. But nothing will ever be routine for me now.

I pull out my maths book, but the figures, the equations, float away to their own unreachable universe. My phone beeps. I pull it out and check the message. *Happy birthday kiddo.* I turn my phone off.

More kids jump on the bus in succession, yelling greetings and thumping their bodies and bags into the seats around me. Every shrill voice, every bump in the road jars. Kyra, a girl from my Maths and English Lit classes sits next to me.

"Hi."

"Hi."

That's as far as our conversation goes. She turns to chat to two girls sitting behind us. I know them by name, Caitlin and Lana. I'm too numb to think about joining in, so I close my eyes, but the images there are bad, so I open my eyes again to stare at the roadside, the bush, the morning sun turning the clouds deep pink. Shepherd's warning.

—◦—

The bell for first class rings as I'm standing at my locker. I can't do it. I can't sit in a classroom full of chattering, whingeing kids and pretend everything is okay. I rest my head on the ledge of my locker.

"Are you okay?" someone asks. It's Kyra from the bus.

"I'm okay."

"You sure?"

I nod.

"You don't want to be late for the maths exam."

Crap. How could I have forgotten? "I won't."

As she hurries off, I realise my hands are shaking. Two words keep coming at me: tell someone. It's the right thing to do. But I know what will happen. I've seen enough cop shows. Hell itself will come to visit. Doctors will have me lying open and naked, probing my soreness, police will descend on the house – their fellow cop's house – endless questions will be asked. Would they even believe me? I imagine the headlines: Retired Cop Rapes Stepdaughter. Only he didn't ... did he? Not really. What do you even call it? It felt like rape.

The corridor is empty now. I close my locker and take a few steps towards my classroom.

Tell someone.

What about Mum? What will happen to her? What will happen to me? But if I don't tell, who's to say it won't happen again? This thought jolts me.

———◆◇◆———

The lady at the office says the school counsellor is taking a class right now, but then she looks at me closely and her expression changes. My eyes must look like crap. They sting. They're probably all red from no sleep. She says to wait. I sit in the hall, on an orange plastic chair, my books tightly clenched to my chest, my feet and knees pressed together. Am I really doing this? Will they believe me?

There's a boy in town who had some sort of brain cancer. He walked around for weeks with his head in bandages and everybody pretended they didn't see them, but they made a big deal of shaking his hand, cooing over his bravery, looking everywhere but at the elephant-in-the-room cloth that wound around his head like a turban. He's better now, but people still refer to him as "Cancer Boy'.

"Hello, I'm Margaret Carmody. Did you want to talk to me?"

I purse my lips. This is a mistake.

"What's your name?" she asks.

I shake my head.

"Okay, well ... how about you come with me and we can have a chat in private?"

"No, it's okay. I was feeling a bit sick, but I feel better now."

She crosses her arms, frowning. "You don't look fine."

I shrug. "I am."

She squats in front of me and puts her hands on my knees. I jump. She takes them away. "Sweetheart, if you don't want to talk it's okay. But let's go to the sick bay, and we'll have the nurse take a look at you. To make sure."

I swallow and nod. I don't know what else to do.

She asks me to sit on the sick bay stretcher while she fetches the nurse. My head pounds, blood rushing faster every second I wait. Closing my eyes doesn't help. It makes it worse, more intense.

What am I going to say? I think he raped me? But not really. He couldn't... get it in, but it hurt. I think maybe he was too drunk, or I was too tense, or maybe he never meant for it to go that far. And I've showered and washed. There's no proof of what he left all over me. And who are they going to believe? Trusty Samuel who's been in the police force since forever, who's been looking after his poor, sick wife? Or me. A kid. Maybe they'll think I'm after attention.

I get off the stretcher. Need to get out of here. The school library is the only escape I can think of, a retreat, somewhere to think clearly. I don't want to be known as "Rape Girl".

———◆———

The librarian must be taking a toilet break. I head to a desk up the back, behind the shelves, so she can't spot me when she returns. My eyes are too tired to read, my head too busy to think.

It's now I remember Harry's text and pull my phone out. It beeps several times when I turn it on, and I panic, turning the volume down. Harry has been persistent:

Hello birthday girl.

Hello?

Speak!

Talk to me!

Arrgghh fail! Just realised your bday was yest. Forgive?

I stare at the two lines of smiley emoticons that follow. What do I say back? "Sorry for slow response. Busy being raped". I laugh at myself, but it's not funny, it's hatred. Instead I text:

Fine

I sag when I realise all the implications that word carries. And then I stop caring because it's too fucking hard, and things *are* fine. They're just fucking fine. I turn the phone off again, fold my arms on the desk and rest my head.

Sometime later, the school bell jerks me awake. I sit, blurry, waiting to see if any students enter the library. It's quiet. I rest my head again, but I can't sleep. I pick up my books and leave. I need to smash something.

10

Rigor Mortis

Our front gate creaks like it always does. The gravel crunches. The miniature windmill that sits on our roof drifts lazily round and round. Same. Same. Same. Except the air is cooler. Summer's done a runner while I was at school.

The front door is unlocked, just as I left it. I push it open. It's still hot in the house. As I step inside, the fear I've been holding back with my anger unnerves me. My hands shake. I don't let them stop me. I dump my bag inside my bedroom door, like I always do, and pause to lean against the wall.

Trouble breathing. My adrenaline is surging from the enormity of what I'm about to do. Confront him. Tell him what he's done is unforgivable. That if he touches me again, I will kill him. I clench my teeth. Come on. You can do this. You did it when you were ten, so you can do it now. I wish my body would listen to my brain.

Mum is sitting at the kitchen table, still in her nightie. She has an arm wrapped defensively around a bucket of melted ice cream. A milky mess dribbles down her wrist from the wooden spoon she holds.

"I was hungry," she says.

"Where's Samuel?"

She shakes her head. "Gone."

"Where?"

"Gone." She dives the spoon into the ice cream, then sucks at it.

I leave her there and head to the backyard. No sign of him. He can't be far; his car is in the drive. Don't tell me he hasn't bothered getting up yet?

The bedroom stinks of sweat, bad breath and something else. There he is, lying face down, naked on the bed covers. I don't turn away this time. Instead, I stare in disgust. Too fucking lazy to get up and look after his own wife.

"You're revolting," I yell. "You're filthy. You're an arsehole!"

I wait for him to wake up, to try and make groggy excuses. If he apologises, I won't accept it. I'll tell him he's going to jail. I'll tell him he's going to rot there.

"GET UP!"

He doesn't budge. It's now, while my heart is hammering and my breath is coming in angry gulps, I notice his strange colour.

⊰◦⊱

Mary is rocking me like a baby as we sit in the lounge, curtains drawn against the prying eyes of curious neighbours.

"It's okay, it's okay," she coos.

But it isn't.

My head is numb. It's as if my mouth has been glued shut, and I've got all these words inside that are so jumbled I don't know how to get them out. I think I'm crying; the tears dribbling from my chin are coming from somewhere.

What happens now? They've taken Mum to the hospice. That much I know. Mary is saying I can stay with her and Fred. They have a spare room. They'll look after me. The men are carrying Samuel's body out. It takes three of them because he's so big.

Mary tries to turn my head, to shield me. "Don't look, sweetie."

But I do. I want to see for myself if his face is covered like a dead person's. I can't – they've put him inside a large blue zip-up bag. Will he be buried like that? Like a nothing? Like a no-one?

I want to be the one to throw the first piece of dirt on his casket. I picture myself holding a big clod of muddy earth in my fist and throwing it into his open grave. Not dropping it, not letting it fall from my hand, but throwing it. Hard.

And this is the thought that makes the pain start in my chest. A huge, hiccupping pain, wrenching more tears from me. And I don't know why. Didn't he deserve to die for what he did? To me. To Mum. Isn't he a coward, taking the easy way out like that and leaving us to fend for ourselves? He doesn't deserve my tears.

11

Abjuration

Nine o'clock on the dot, the doorbell rings. I'm in Mary's spare bedroom, buried under the doona, trying to keep the world at bay. If I don't get up, I won't have to face anyone. The questions. The sympathetic looks. The knowing looks.

The pink and white pyjamas, which Mary laid out for me last night, are still lying across the foot of the bed, crumpled like a deflated person. I refused to put them on, choosing to stay fully clothed because... just because.

Muffled voices, then footsteps as Mary leads the visitors down the hall into the lounge room. I don't know how, maybe it's Mary's sombre tone, but I'm sure it's the police.

Mary taps on my door. "Lauren?"

I drag myself out of bed without answering.

She enters the room and glances at my crumpled clothes, smiles sadly as she attempts to tidy my hair, brushing it behind my ears and flattening the flyaways, all the while telling me I shouldn't be frightened. Everyone is on my side. Everyone wants to support me. I follow her to the lounge room and stand, zombie-like, waiting for more instructions.

Fred is sitting on the couch, while two police officers stand by. A male and a female. The lady officer suggests we go into the kitchen to talk.

Mary puts her hand on my shoulder. "It's okay if I stay with her?"

The policewoman nods. "Yes, of course. We require a parent or guardian to be present."

"Good," says Mary. "I'll make a cuppa. You boys want one?"

The policewoman and I sit at the table while Mary puts the kettle on, then leans against the kitchen sink. The policewoman tells me her name is Sophie and that she's very sorry for what's happened.

I shrug. Whatever. I pick at my thumbnail, which is infinitely more interesting. Or distracting. Or something.

"Lauren, I want you to know that nothing you say will get you into trouble. Okay?" Her words have the opposite effect: it feels as if I'm on trial.

I shrug.

She starts by asking how I am. I try to answer, but my throat is claggy, as if I haven't used my voice in a week. "Okay." It seems a ridiculous answer when I know I look like crap. But it's one those "How-are-you – I'm-fine' things.

"I need to ask you a few things to clarify the circumstances of Samuel's death."

I nod.

She asks me a bunch of questions that seem obvious to me. Where I'd been that day, what time I left school, what time I found Samuel. I answer mechanically, transferring my picking to a loose thread on Mary's cotton tablecloth. Then the hard part starts.

"Lauren, did you know that Samuel left a letter?"

I breathe deep through my nose, nod.

"And do you know what was in it?"

I shake my head. It's true, I don't. I look up, frightened. Did Samuel confess in that letter? I search her face. Her gaze is soft but unwavering. I flick my eyes back to the tablecloth. Surely, it's a suicide note? She's already told me his cause of death is likely too many sleeping pills combined with alcohol. Surely, he hasn't betrayed me a second time?

"Is there anything you want to tell me?"

My thoughts churn. How much does she know? "Can I see it?"

"It's still considered evidence."

I try to act as though it's no big deal. But what's he written?

"Lauren, it's okay. You can tell me. Nothing here is your fault. I'm here to help you."

God. Don't cry. Do. Not. Cry.

She touches my arm, making me look up again. Sympathy covers every inch of her face, as if she thinks I'm some injured fledgling who's fallen out of its nest. *Does* she know? She can't. Otherwise she'd be offering me counselling, a doctor, a rape test or *something*.

"Lauren, was Samuel upset about something? Did something happen?"

I shake my head again. "I don't know. No. Everything was fine."

"He wasn't depressed about something? About your mum?"

And there's my out. "I guess he was down about Mum getting worse. About retiring."

"Okay. I noticed a lot of beer bottles in the lounge. Did he drink that much often?"

"Yes. All the time." And there's my first lie to the law.

"I see. Now Lauren. I need to ask you this. It's not pleasant, but we have to know."

I clench my teeth. I haven't escaped yet.

"Did Samuel hurt you in any way? Did he touch you in a way that made you feel uncomfortable?"

"No." My second lie. It comes so easily, it surprises me.

She pauses then and pulls a piece of paper from her notes. "Okay, just a couple more questions."

I chew my lip, relieved it's nearly over.

"Lauren, sometimes things happen that are hard to talk about. Things that might feel shameful."

I can't help myself. The words spring out before I think. "Did he say he did something?"

"Well, no, but—"

"Because nothing happened. I don't know what you're talking about." I clamp my mouth shut. God, I must sound so guilty. I press down my panic. Breathe. Breathe. "I wish you'd leave me alone." I turn away, praying she'll go back to her police business and let me go back to bed. We should all just forget everything. It would be so much easier.

She takes a breath and tries again. "Lauren. I know you're angry. You must be feeling hurt—"

Her words are kerosene to my sparking embers. Suddenly I'm a furnace. "I'm not! Nothing happened. I came home and found him dead. He killed himself. I don't care. And I don't care what he said in his letter. It's nothing to do with me."

Her attention is unwavering, suffocating. I can't breathe. She puts her hand on my arm. I shake her off.

"Lauren... I know it's hard—"

"You don't know anything!"

"Yes, yes I do."

And when I look at her, ready to spitfire again, I know she's telling the truth. Somewhere in her eyes, I can tell she knows exactly how I feel. And it terrifies me. I'm not ready for this. I'm not ready to share how disgusting I am. How this is my fault too, not just Samuel's. I knew things weren't right between us. I shouldn't have let him close. I should have screamed, I should have fought, torn at him, kicked and punched.

My anger drains as quickly as it flared. Utter tiredness overtakes me. "Are we done?"

"Okay, Lauren. I'll leave my card in case—"

"Thanks."

Trembling, I get up and walk as calmly as I can out the back door. I sit on the porch trying to catch my breath. *Hold it together. Wait until they've gone.*

And I do. I compact my fear, my anger, my doubt, all of it, deep inside, and I picture my out-of-control emotions solidifying into a hard, tight nugget that one day I'll spit out and never have to deal with again.

Later, at night, when tears threaten, I bite down on my arm until the pain numbs me. In the morning, I'm careful to hide the marks and bruises. And the other letter they don't know about.

Mary bought me this diary.

She says anything I find too hard to say, I can write in here. No-one has the right to read it, unless I want them to.

I've got nothing to say.

12

Lassitude

I'm on Mary's back porch. Golds and browns are creeping into the fruit tree leaves, and the last summer tomatoes, full and overripe, are barely clinging to their vines. I sit on a padded bench with a book on my lap. It's been open at the same page for hours.

"Sweetie?" Mary calls. I hear her huffs from the driveway before she appears. The knee-high grass growing against the back of the house catches my attention as she brushes past it. Fred and Mary are not that keen on gardening, apart from their practical fruits and veg. Samuel would never have let the grass get that long. A fire hazard, he would have said. Ugh. It bugs me when thoughts of him invade my head like that.

Mary groans as she stomps her cankles up the few steps of the porch. She's been to the letterbox. "This came for you." She holds her arm out, the skin underneath wobbling as she brandishes an envelope. I swear she gets bigger by the day, and I think about telling her she needs to lay off the scones and cream cakes she's constantly trying to cram down my throat.

"Sweetie, you're losing too much weight," she says, pouting when I refuse to touch more than a few mouthfuls of soup.

But I don't say anything, because her weight is none of my business, and she's been so kind to me, and why am I such a bitch?

I know I should eat. I know I should do something about my straggly hair. I know I should go back to school. But my bones feel so heavy I can't make them go any further than the porch. I don't even have the energy to push a few buttons to respond to Harry's text messages. I close my eyes, weary at the thought of the effort required.

"Here," says Mary. "It's from the police."

My heart constricts as she hands me the letter. Samuel's handwriting on the front is succinct:

To: Wineera Police

From: Samuel H Barnes

"They said you can have it," says Mary. "They've finished with it. But I don't think it's a good idea." She stands, hands hitched on her hips, looking worried. "You don't have to read it if you don't want to. You know ... if you think it'll be too upsetting ..."

I turn the envelope over, pretend I haven't seen it before, that it wasn't lying next to the letter addressed to me, in the same type of envelope. Samuel's name and address are typeset on the back in a curvy font – a present from Mum. At the time she gave them to him, I wondered, Who writes letters these days? I guess he finally got some use out of them. The top edge is ragged where a police officer has torn it open. How much has Samuel said?

Mary eases herself onto the bench and lays her hands on her apron-covered lap. "Do you want me to read it for you?"

I shake my head. "No." Nausea creeps into my belly as I slip the letter out of its envelope and read.

I am solely responsible for my own death.

I am solely to blame.

Samuel's signature is scrawled beneath. I show the letter to Mary who huffs. "That's it? I don't understand. It's cryptic."

It's not cryptic to me. The real message will be in the other letter. But I'm not ready for that yet. I fold the letter back into the envelope, place it between the pages of my book and close the cover. Mary puts her arm around my shoulders. She can comfort me all she likes. I'm done crying.

13

Acquiescence

I sniff and screw up my nose. The air smells like an op shop that's been sprayed with air freshener – a lingering, stale, soupy smell but with a sweet aftertaste. I spot Mum in the common area. She isn't hard to find; only five other residents are in the room.

She's sitting in a faded floral easy chair by the window. Floral to match the curtains, the cushions, the sofas. Someone must have been having a fire sale on chintz – I think that's what they call it – back when the hospice was built. A lump has formed in my throat, and I fight back a sudden sadness. It's May, almost three months since I've seen her. She's way too young to be stuck among all these grannies whose use-by dates are almost expired.

Mum turns to me when I sit next to her. No recognition, a flat expression. God, how has she aged so quickly? The deepened lines, thinning hair, watery eyes. She looks so much older than her late fifty-something years. She works at turning her wedding ring round and round her finger. Always busy hands. They shake now. Her eternity ring is missing – the white-gold one Samuel gave her when she turned the big 5-0.

Mum wasn't happy when he presented it. She said it would have cost a fortune and the money could have been spent better elsewhere. Samuel huffed and told her to enjoy it. It was pretty, with a small diamond in claws, and three inset sapphires either side. I hope it's not lost. Perhaps it's sitting in her jewellery box back home. *Home.* I have to get used to not having one anymore. I can't go back there, not on my own. Not that I'd want to after …

I give Mum a kiss on the cheek, which she accepts before turning her head back to the window. I pick up her hand. Her skin is dry and papery, and I make a mental note to bring her some moisturiser.

"Mum? How are you?"

She starts humming. Or maybe she was already humming, but I haven't noticed.

"Mum? I'm sorry I haven't come sooner. I needed some time—"

She turns and pats my hand. "Yes. Yes."

"How are things? Are they treating you well?"

"Yes. Yes. Good. Good." She takes her hand back and points. "But look at Bert. He shouldn't be weeing on the garden like that."

"Bert' is actually someone's grandpa who's dribbling against a window and making a finger-paint picture with his saliva.

"He's not weeing, Mum. He's... drawing."

"No. He's weeing. I've told them before, but they won't listen."

"He's spitting, Mum. Not quite as gross—"

"He's not! Don't speak to me like I'm an idiot. I can see quite clearly what he's doing."

"Okay," I say, pursing my lips.

She nods, apparently satisfied.

"Don't worry about it," I add.

"Well, I won't if you won't, but he's going to kill the garden."

I'm relieved if that's all she's worried about. Not Samuel's death or her own deterioration. I don't think we'll be having conversations about either of those horrors now or in the future. I'd rather she lives in whatever world gives her peace. Outside the window, there's nothing but grass. Autumn grass. Growing while it still can, before winter rolls in and stunts it.

<hr>

I'm cold all the time. My bones ache as though I have the flu. I feel old, decrepit. I migrate to Mary's front veranda. It's a bright day. Blue skies. Maybe the winter sun will thaw me a tiny bit. No luck, it's too weak, and the chill pries its way through every stitch of my jumper. Yet, I stay. Something is clawing at my insides.

Across the road, three doors down, our house – Samuel's house – seems dead. There's no smoke from the chimney. Weeds are sprouting through the rockery. The nature strip, once pristine in Samuel's determination to show he was coping, is overgrown.

The screen door bangs before I notice Mary with a toasted sandwich and mug of hot chocolate. She's even got mini marshmallows floating in it. "How are you? Ooh, it's freezing out here." She sets the food on a little table next to me. "Please try to eat something. You missed lunch." She shudders and rubs her arms. "Are you sure you don't want to come inside?"

"No. The sun is nice."

"Okay. The air will do you good, I guess." She reaches into her pocket. "Another letter from the lawyers." She holds it out to me, but I look away. "I'll read it for you, shall I?"

She takes a seat and skims the letter. "It's legalese, but I'll try to pick out the important bits." She sniffs and pushes her reading glasses up her nose. I tune out because the sniffing and glasses habit thing annoys me. And my annoyance annoys me because Mary is so good to me. I have these moments where I hate everything and everybody. Maybe that's what's making me feel so ill. I hate me too.

She's talking. "… deceased estate … probate … claimants … mental capacity …' She scratches her head, and I almost laugh because she looks like such a grandmotherly cliché. Then I feel sorry for myself because I never had a grandmother.

"Okay," she says. "Here's the upshot: Samuel's estate goes to your mum, and her estate goes to you once she's incapable of making rational decisions. I think we're way past that point."

"Hmm."

"The lawyers will remain trustees of the estate until you turn eighteen."

"Uh huh."

"They want to discuss rental of the property in the meantime, and what to do with all the personal and household goods."

I'm not ready for that. I don't think I ever will be. "They can do whatever they like," I say. "It can burn down for all I care."

Mary sighs. "It'll get better, sweetie."

"Mmmm."

She gets up and straightens her apron. I hate that stupid apron with its bright orange apples and blue leaves. Did she get it at a discount because someone stuffed up the colours?

Stop. I need to stop.

"I agree with them cutting off the utilities for now," she says. "What's the point of paying bills when no-one's living there?"

She stretches, then dawdles, looking as if she wants to ask something else. I'm pretty sure I know what it is. I'm right.

"Have you thought any more about going back to school? Your studies and schoolmates might be a good distraction for you."

I scrunch down into the corner of my bench, and as I do, I spot a car approaching. I expect it to slow as it passes Samuel's house. It doesn't. The rubberneckers seem to have dwindled at last, no longer walking or driving out of their way to see the house where someone killed themselves. The way they had skulked through, you'd think the place was a museum, or a sideshow attraction. Like there was something ghoulish behind those lace curtains.

Mary misinterprets my reaction. "I'll get you a blanket. You're freezing, poor thing."

Once I'm alone, the house seems to glare at me. Why would I want the place anyway? Especially now. It's only a pile of weatherboards. A box of horrible. Still, it sits there like a taunt, silently daring me to come back.

14

Coercion

Winter. I've missed nearly the whole second term of school. What's the point of continuing? Mary's patience has worn off. "You can't sit around the house all day. I know it's been hard, awful, but it's time."

I ignore her, throw a tantrum, refuse to eat, but she won't budge. Finally, she gives me a choice: attend counselling or face the music.

I chicken out and choose the music.

My first class is unbearable. I sit there, sick at how much I've missed. I'm never going to catch up. Never going to pass my VCE. At least the teacher doesn't draw attention to me, and there's only the occasional whisper and glance. Not unexpected – I have been absent after all. People are bound to talk.

Then comes the second class.

"So sorry for your loss, Lauren. Must have been horrible, you poor thing."

It's Bria Thompson – petite, clear-skinned and straight-haired – who's never spoken to me in her entire life, apart from the glare she gave me when Harry and I beat her in the school music comp. That look spoke loads. She sidles into the spare seat at my desk and pats my arm.

I steel myself for the inevitable. "Thanks. I'm okay. You needn't bother."

"I can't imagine what you've been through."

No, she can't. No-one can. I glance towards the open door, hoping our teacher will make a sudden appearance. Not likely, Mrs Skarton always arrives at the last second. I don't blame her; I'm wishing I'd waited myself.

I shrug.

Bria sighs. "You poor thing. Where are you living now?"

I consider ignoring her but figure if I answer she might go away.

"The Worthingtons' place."

"Old Mary's? Poor thing."

I'm not sure if I'm still the poor thing, or Mary. Whatever, I wish she'd disappear. Something tells me she isn't being Florence Nightingale.

She leans in, whispers. I don't have to look at her to know she's smirking. "Did you see him die? I've never seen a dead person."

A rolling anger whooshes up and my chair clatters over backwards as I shoot to my feet. "Back off, bitch!"

Bria gets up from her chair, startled but smirking. "Touchy, aren't we?"

"I'll give you touchy." I draw myself up into someone bigger and stronger than I feel. I have no idea if I'm capable of beating her – she's taller than me – but I imagine springing at her, like a wildcat, our arms, legs and long hair flailing on the floor between the desks, and me smashing her pretty face in.

Mrs Skarton's shrill voice cuts through. "What's going on?"

"Nothing," Bria says. She slinks away to another seat.

Mrs Skarton looks at me carefully. "Are you alright, Lauren?"

What I want to say is, if people would leave me alone, stop asking, I'd be fine. What I do say is, "Perfect."

It could have been worse. Much worse, if Bria knew the whole story.

I try to settle down and listen to what the teacher is saying, but my mind is a jumble, my whole body tense – a radar for murmurs and giggles. A dropped pencil makes my head spin. A chair scrape is like fingernails on the blackboard. God, I hope it isn't always going to be like this.

The next class, after recess, word of the Bria altercation seems to have spread, and I'm pretty much left alone. Good. If they're scared off, that's fine with me.

❦

The morning drags into lunchtime. I sit on the bench Harry and I used to share, even though it's a wet, miserable day and my feet are frozen. I check my phone for messages. There's a missed call and two texts from Harry. I ignore them, guilty because now Mary has been bugging me to call him back.

"You two used to be so close. It's a shame to let it go."

I wish *she* would let it go. I put the phone back in my pocket. Drizzle threatens, so I pull the hood of my jacket up. It sucks, but it's better than being in the common room where everyone can stare. Mary's ham and pickle sandwich sits in a piece of tin foil on my lap. It's bald at the edges where I've picked at the crusts.

"Pathetic."

Great. The school's token goth has come to mock me. I know this guy. Well, not *know* him; he was in Harry's year. We've never spoken, but he catches my school bus, and you can't miss him – his angular face and kohl-rimmed eyes. Striking really, along with his lithe physique and shards of black hair sticking up, punk-like. Why is he still in school? Didn't he graduate? And why do some people feel the need to shove their faces where they don't belong?

I ignore him, focus on my sandwich, but he stands firm, hands on hips, all superior. "I said, you look pathetic."

I relent and give him my best glare. "I'm not biting. Go be a dick to someone else."

"Huh! I wish. You have no idea."

"Yeah, well, neither do you, so how about you go do your goth act somewhere else?"

"But I do know. You're every wimpy kid who's ever let life smack them to the ground. Look at you. You're a senior, and you still haven't figured out how to stick up for yourself, poor kitten."

Who the hell? I look at him properly now. What's his name? Greg, Gary, George or something ... yes, this is the guy who won the school comp with his drag act last year. Brave, considering he was only new to the school. "I remember you."

He spreads his arms as if he's about to take a bow ... or take flight. "Ah, the penny's dropped. You and me, honey. We're not so different."

Unbelievable. Does he want to join forces and start a glee club? "I'm not into pity parties. Go find someone else."

"Sweetie, you *are* a pity party. All on your lonesome in the cold. Poor kitten."

I stare daggers at him. Enough with the *poor kitten*. I'm not a kitten. I'm not poor. What I am is in need of a punching bag, and if he isn't careful, he might end up filling that role.

He sits next to me, bumping me with his butt. "Scooch over. I'm here to rescue this drowning kitty."

"Oh what? Get real." I thump his butt back with mine. "And get lost."

"Is that all you've got?" He bumps me harder and my sandwich slips off my lap, splatting on the asphalt at my feet.

"You bastard!" I turn and shove him with both hands. "Fuck off! I don't need you. I don't need anyone. Take your bloody sympathy somewhere else."

He lands on his bum on the wet ground, shocked, then laughs as he gets up and brushes himself off. "Now *that's* what I'm talking about." He takes his seat again. "I knew you had it in you."

"So, you're a button pusher. Great. Just what I need."

"You so do."

He holds his hand out. It looks smooth, manicured even. "Snap's the name. And Kitten, I'm one hundred per cent gay, not goth."

I hesitate. I've never been up close to a gay before … that I know of. Does he think I'm gay too? Is that what he means by *we're not so different*? "What kind of a name is Snap?"

He sighs, bored. "Got it in primary school, when we lived in Sydney. I snapped my teacher's bra."

"That couldn't have had a happy ending."

"No. But it was worth it. The cow."

Curious, I shake his hand. "I'm not a lesbian."

He laughs so hard I think he's going to fall off the bench again. "Come on, let's ditch your sad sandwich and get some hot soup at the cafeteria. We'll turn this soggy kitty into a tiger."

———◆———

I met someone today. His name is Snap.
He's weird, pushy, but I like him.

15

Collusion

I'm not sure if it's hunger making my stomach gurgle or if it's nerves from what I'm about to tell Snap. I place my order with Trish – toasted banana bread – then wait for her to be out of earshot. Here goes nothing. Snap is staring out the café window, so I tap the table to get his attention.

"I'm thinking about leaving. Going to Melbourne. Or Sydney."

Snap bangs his Coke down on the table, sending fizz everywhere. "Holy shit!" He grabs some napkins and dabs at his lap, his hand, the table. "When did this decision cross your pretty little mind?"

"This morning. While I was brushing my teeth."

"Always the best time for making decisions. Hell, Kitten. Let's do it."

"What?"

Snap grins. "I'm with you."

"Really?"

"Really. This town sucks balls like a hairy dog."

I scrunch up my face. Sometimes he creates pictures in my head that can't be unimagined. A partner in crime? I like the idea but ... "We hardly know each other."

Snap rolls his Malteser-brown eyes. "Honey, we're not getting married. We're reaching into our futures, setting our sights on something better. The big-wide-world better. Besides, who ever really *knows* anyone?"

Good point. But all I know about him is what he's told me over the past three weeks: he lives two and a half blocks from me; he's repeating his final year to piss off his homophobic dad; and he's as miserable as I am, only he doesn't wear it on his sleeve like I do – he'd rather wear red leather pants, silk shirts and a jacket with a rainbow unicorn on the back. He doesn't though, because he'd get beaten up. Instead, he protests by wearing all black.

Still, this is serious. I haven't really thought about the future, only getting away from here. Anyway, who said I'd made a decision? I said I was thinking about leaving.

Snap's a mind reader. "We can always finish school later. Think of it as a gap year."

"And your parents really wouldn't care?"

"Parent. Singular. Mum's dead. And honey, my dad would pack my bags and pay my fare to the moon if I asked. As far as he's concerned, getting this godless homo out of his blessed house would be a win."

I smile even though what he's said is awful. Together we're a bad statistic. Ha. I've learnt something from Sociology class. Perhaps somewhere out there, in the land of happy families, are perfect parents who support Vegemite-cheeked children and love them, no matter how they grow up. Good on you Mr and Mrs Brady. Good on you Modern Family – yell at each other, misunderstand each other, but at the end of the day you're still there, and would kill for each other. Not kill yourself.

"He says that soon as I've finished school, I'm out anyway."

"That's so unfair."

"Welcome to my world. But look who's talking. Only difference is your dad took himself out of the picture. You should feel blessed."

"What? You'd feel better if your dad killed himself?"

Snap stares at me. Too long. He's trying to decide something. I squirm. "What?"

He rolls up one of his sleeves and holds his arm out to me. Embedded in his skin are rows and rows of thin lines. There must be at least forty or fifty. Neat rows and criss-crosses. Some are fresh, raised and angry, and others are faded as if they've healed a while ago.

I can't help staring at them. I almost reach to touch them but hold back. It feels too personal.

"It's the only way I can block out his lectures, his hate talk. He thinks he can brainwash me into being straight."

What a dick. "God, I'm so sorry. Does ... does he hit you?"

Snap looks away, jaw tightening. I hope it's not worse. He turns back and laughs. "Not anymore. He's in a wheelchair now. Fell off his pulpit. The great Demitrius Theodakis can't catch me now!"

I don't know what to say. "Snap, why haven't you left?"

He sighs. "I don't know. Guilt? He's still my dad. And he's got too much pride to accept help from his mates."

I think of Samuel. What is it with these guys? I bite down on my lip, because it seems like one of those moments where I should share something of myself, so Snap doesn't feel alone, so we don't have to be the only members of our exclusive hate clubs. I know he's the kind of person to keep a secret, and it'd be so good to know someone understands ... but I can't do it. I've tied my knot too hard.

"TMI?" He looks crestfallen as he pulls his sleeve back down. I can't tell if he's faking it or not.

"No. I'm glad you showed me."

"DIY tatts, I call it. It's all the rage." He laughs again, and there's his wall back up. I've missed my opportunity. "Guess your dad did a better job of it than me," he adds.

I suck in my breath. "You weren't really trying to kill yourself?"

"Nah. He's not worth it."

"Good. And Samuel was my *step*father," I say. "Now he's one *step* closer to heaven. Or hell maybe." I'm trying to sound flippant, but it's coming out all awkward and stupid. Why can't I nail that? Lately everything I say sounds like a whinge. I change tack. "What happened to your mum?"

"Died of a broken heart."

"What? Seriously?"

"No. Cancer." He laughs again.

"That's not funny." He's exhausting.

"Kitten, my life is one big joke. Get over it. So, curiosity got the cat – what happened to your real dad? You never told me."

"You never asked."

"Oh, poor pet." He tries to stroke my hair, but I brush him off.

"Get stuffed."

He softens. "I'm asking now."

"He rolled his tractor, and it crushed him." I flinch as I say this. It's been so long, I didn't realise it would still hurt.

"Child! Your family knows how to do drama."

I could slap him. Doesn't he know how hurtful he's being?

"Oh, come on, honey. You gotta laugh at that crapolla, or you'll drown in a sea of self-pity." He drinks the remainder of his Coke, then starts to crush the can on the table. "So, no relatives?"

"Not here. Samuel mentioned people in the UK. Distant relos, I think. We never got Christmas cards or anything."

The Coke can is almost concertinaed. "So, did you inherit property or something?"

"Not from my real dad. Our farm went downhill after he died. We had to sell. Mum said she didn't get much for it. The lawyers say I won't get anything until I'm eighteen, apart from school fees and stuff."

"So, you're a farm girl? Yee ha!"

"Not really."

Snap uses the heel of his hand to push the can into a solid round disc. I wonder at his strength, given he's so skinny. Well, not skinny. Lean, all muscle. "So, let's do this thing!"

"But... what are we going to do for money? Wouldn't it be better to wait until—"

"Are you chickening out on me?"

I shrink into myself like a turtle. "No. Just being practical."

"I've got a stash of guilt money my gran in Melbourne sends me."

"Guilt money?"

"Yeah. Pay off the faggot grandkid, and she never has to see me." He narrows his eyes. "Maybe we should go to Melbourne. Then I can hit her up if we get stuck."

"Maybe." It sounds appealing to have a fallback.

"What about your parents' house?" he asks. "Old folks always have bits of money hidden for emergencies. Or you could sell some stuff. No-one's going to miss it."

"I never thought of that."

"I'm full of good ideas. Besides, the man owes you for making you an orphan."

"I'm not an orphan. My mum's still alive."

"Just."

Ouch. It's going to take a while to get used to his too honest, too cutting quips. But he's right. Mum seems to have lost touch with reality for good now, idling her time away in her chair by the window. It's depressing. She hardly recognises me. I may as well be an orphan. And Snap's right again: Samuel does owe me. Again, I'm thinking about letting Snap in. Is it time to unburden?

Nothing gets by him. "What's simmering behind those beautiful angry eyes of yours?" He winks with a you-can-tell-me expression. God, he's good at that: flicking between flippant and friend. "I told you we're not that different," he adds.

I can't do it. I change the subject. "You're serious? We're really going to do this?"

"You betcha."

"So how do we start?"

"Okay, step one. You got any ID?"

"What for?"

He taps my head. "Think, Kitten, think. Little things like renting an apartment, getting a licence or whatever. Trust me, it'll make your life so much easier. You got a birth certificate or something?"

"All that stuff is still in the house." Geez, Snap is smart. I'd never have thought about things like this.

"Okay, you need to get that. Step two, money."

"So, taking stuff from the house. Wouldn't that be stealing?"

Snap's eyes glint. "Not if no-one knows about it. It's all yours when you turn eighteen anyway, yeah? What's the big deal? You're just cashing in early."

I sit back and contemplate the ceiling so I can think without looking at him. There's a dusty bit of web, high in one corner. I wonder where its owner has gone. It reminds me of Harry's porch – the little spider that kept rebuilding. Did this one give up?

I breathe in deeply, then let it all out in a soundless whistle. A few minutes ago, this was only musings. How did it suddenly get so real? Do I go? Or do I stay here where memories are always going to slam me in the face? Where I have to always hide part of myself? Where no-one gets me because I can't let them?

I pick up the remains of Snap's Coke can. The thin aluminium walls have been crushed into something strong and immovable.

"Guess I'm going to have to go a-visiting."

It can't hurt you. It can't hurt you. It can't hurt you. Three. Isn't that the magic number for incantations? My hand is resting on the gate, its metal coils cold under my palm. The house. Not much has changed, except the windows have grown a gauzy skin of dust, and nightshade plants with their toxic berries are popping up everywhere. And the lavender bushes have gone all leggy. That's what Mum used to call it. I remember asking her how plants could have legs. And if they did, why didn't they get up and run away? I'll never hear that laugh again.

I push the gate open, strangely comforted by its ever-present creak. Spell *perennial*. I close the gate and walk down the driveway. Samuel's car has bird poop down its tailgate.

I have every right to be here. But if I believe that, why haven't I told Mary? I put my hand on my belly, telling my stomach to relax. Nothing bad is going to happen. There's no-one here.

Just me.

At the side of the house, I pass the concrete tubs where Mum's day lilies are dying off, their leaves yellow and saggy as though they're depressed. There's Samuel's shed where he once tried to brew beer. The bottles exploded in sticky cascades. And the rosebush, its thorns exposed and prominent now that its leaves have dropped. How many times have I caught my jumper, or scratched my bare arms on it, and cursed? Smith is buried there, his little bones curled up in an eternal catnap.

Who cares if someone sees me? What can they do? Wave a finger? Besides, I can say I've come to collect some of my belongings. Which is true.

As I round the back of the house, a dripping noise tells me the water tank is overflowing. Clean fresh water going to waste. Samuel would be annoyed.

The screen door gives a telling click, then another as the lock disengages. My heart lurches knowing there's nothing stopping me now, except I can't shake the feeling I'm about to walk on someone's grave.

The stench hits me as soon as I push the back door open. God, hasn't anybody thought to open the windows and doors? Are the same soiled sheets and covers still lying on Samuel's bed?

I pull my jumper over my nose, ready to fight down whatever horrors my imagination can dig up. But it's too much. I back out, fall to my knees on the grass and heave my guts up. In a while, I wipe my face on my jumper sleeve, get up and sit on the porch swing.

Breathe. Breathe. Breathe.

Eyes closed, I picture Mum here, lying back, feet up and humming some tune I never could recognise. She won't be coming back. Not to this house. Not to me. Not to herself.

Defeated, I pull out my phone and text Snap:

Can't do it.

Snap: *You want me to come with?*

My thumb pauses: *Tonight?*

Snap: *K* ☺

The phone dings again as I'm about to put it back in my pocket. It's Harry. *How's things? Why aren't you talking to me? Spell "perturbed".*

What do I say? Great to hear from you. Life has gone down one huge toilet since you left. Thanks for not coming back for the funeral.

Selfish, I know. He's busy with uni and everything. But Melbourne's not the other side of the freakin' world. Was one day too much to ask? My stepfather died. That's big, isn't it? In the scale of things that happen in a girl's life? I flick through his other messages and delete them.

Out the front, a neighbour two houses away is raking leaves on her nature strip. She waves. I wave back. She continues her work. I have a sudden urge to visit Mum.

16

Exculpation

Mum is sitting in the same chair, by the same window. There's spittle gathering in the corners of her mouth. Her hands are rubbing up and down her thighs, and she's holding a conversation with someone only her mind can see. She sounds like she used to when she was on the phone to one of her Ladies Auxiliary buddies, talking about cakes for a stall or how to raise money for some poor sod who recently lost his wife. I wonder where she thinks she is.

The smell of the hospice isn't sticking in my nostrils as much today. Maybe it's because nothing could smell as bad as Samuel's house. I sit next to Mum, watching her. Half an hour goes past. I'm trying to memorise her. This might be the last time I see her. Ever. Maybe I shouldn't tell her I'm leaving. Would it be kinder? I mean, who am I doing this for? Her or me? Even if by some miracle she understands, there's nothing she can do about it ... and it might leave her upset. *If* she remembers.

"... and she won't put the blue on the quilt because it won't match the daisies."

I have no idea who "she" is, or what quilt she's talking about.

A buzzer sounds and an attendant comes around announcing dinnertime. I should have come earlier. I forgot they have their evening meal so early. I need to do this in private, not at a table surrounded by elderly citizens who speak too loudly and stare too hard.

Mum's pushing up from her seat, so I grab her hand to help. Food. She's still fixated on it. It's as important as getting her favourite chair – the nurses say she raises hell if she sees someone else sitting in it. It makes me wonder what happened to its previous occupant.

"Yes, yes," Mum says, shuffling towards the door.

Still with the yeses.

"Mum, wait. I need to talk to you."

She turns to look at me, then freezes, surprised. Does she know me?

"Mum?"

"Hmmm?" She leans an ear to me, but her eyes are focused on some invisible scene outside the window.

"Mum, can you look at me?"

She turns, eyebrows raised in question. "Yes, yes. What's your name? I can't remember names these days." She taps her head. "Can't remember."

"Mum, it's me, Lauren."

"Oh, my mother's name was Lauren."

"No, Mum. I'm your daughter."

"Is it dinnertime? I thought I heard the bell."

She moves off.

I let her go.

"I love you, Mum."

The room is quiet. The flower patterns on the chairs and couches look as jaded as the wilting residents.

When I get back to Mary's house there's a small parcel waiting for me. It's full of Chupa Chups.

17

Clandestine

Snap's standing at the gate, his shiny padded jacket reflecting the light of the streetlamp, misty clouds of breath dissipating as fast as he breathes them. I cross the road, rubbing my hands together to keep their circulation going.

"Hi," I whisper.

"Hi, yourself."

"Thanks for doing this."

"Didn't have much choice, did I, Miss Scaredy Cat?" He hands me a flashlight and gives my hooded head a quick rub. "Let's do this."

"Wait. I brought some Vicks. Do you want to put some under your nose? It stinks in there. I saw them do it on CSI."

"Sure."

"And do me a favour?"

"Depends."

"There's a bedroom two doors on the right when you go in. Can you close the door?"

He doesn't need to ask. "Sure, Kitten."

Snap takes the kitchen, rifling through drawers and cabinets, looking for money, while I start in the lounge room, where there's a bunch of paperwork stuffed into a bureau. My tension settles; Snap's presence and confidence is comforting, but it's slow going, sorting through old bills, medical forms and reports with one hand and holding the flashlight in the other. I glance at the fireplace. It would be easier and warmer to do this by firelight. I lay the flashlight on the carpet, screw up a pile of old utility bills to use as kindling, then head out the back to grab a few logs.

Snap calls to me. "What are you doing?"

"I'm lighting the fire. It's cold and I can't see."

"Is that smart?"

"I've got the drapes closed." I wait for his response, unsure.

"Okay."

We keep going until after midnight, and I'm wishing we'd brought a thermos with something hot and sweet. I leave the lounge and trace the glow of Snap's light to the kitchen. He sneezes as I enter. He's kneeling on the floor. Drawers, cake tins and boxes are open all over the place.

"Any luck?" I ask.

"A hundred and sixty-four dollars. You?"

"Nup. It's a mess. I thought Samuel would have kept all his stuff meticulously neat."

Snap sniffs. "I guess he didn't get the *order* part of law and order. Maybe you should try the bedroom?"

I shake my head. It only takes him a second to realise what he's said. He gets up and puts his hands on my shoulders. "Leave it to me. You take the dining room. Okay?"

"Do you want some more Vicks?"

It takes us another half-hour of searching before Snap hits the jackpot. "Got it!" he calls from the bedroom. I head towards his voice but pause in the hallway. "Birth certificate," he says, bringing it out to me. "And I found this too. Thought you might want it."

He holds up an old photo. It's Mum and Dad. My real dad. They're standing next to a tractor. Dad has his foot perched against a wheel and his arm wrapped around Mum who's in jeans and t-shirt, her hair in a ponytail. So young. They're both squinting, sunlight in their eyes, happy. "It must be before I came along," I tell Snap. I point to the cattle dog sitting at their feet. "That's Bundy. He died before I was born." I place it carefully in my jacket pocket.

Snap yawns. "I don't think we're going to find anything else. Bedtime."

I yawn in auto response. "Yeah."

He pulls the money out of his pocket. "Here, I found another couple of hundred in your mum's beauty case. Told you old people forget stuff."

"She isn't that old."

"No. Well, you hang on to it. It's yours."

"Thanks. It's not enough though, is it?"

"It's okay, Kitten. I've got plenty for both of us. We can stay in a youth hostel for a few weeks until we get jobs. We'll be alright. You let me know when you want to leave. I'm ready when you are. You want to take Samuel's car or my old bomb?"

I screw up my face. "The bomb? I know Samuel's will be mine eventually, but I don't want to get us charged with car theft in the meantime."

"Done."

"Thanks. Is this Sunday okay? I'm thinking while Mary and Fred are at church ..."

"Sure."

"Okay. You go. I want to finish these last couple of drawers."

Snap folds his arms across his chest. "I'm not leaving you here on your own."

"I lived here, remember? And I'm only a few steps across the road. Go. I'll be fine."

He's not convinced.

"Snap, there's something I want to do before I leave. I want a moment alone to ... say goodbye. You know?"

"Okay." He yawns again and pulls me into a big hug. "Be careful, Kitten." He wipes dust from my face. "Call me if you need me."

I nod.

"Oh, hang on," he says. "I forgot something."

I follow him back to the kitchen where he grabs a packet of Tim Tams. "Waste not, want not," he says. He stops again and points to Samuel's camera sitting on a sideboard. "That's a nice DSLR. Should get a few hundred."

I shake my head. He wrinkles his nose before disappearing.

I go back to the lounge and sit on the floor in front of the fire. Flames still lick at a few pieces of wood, embers glowing strong. It's warm, and I'm satisfied knowing I got what I came for. Except for one thing.

I take the envelope from my back pocket and smooth it over my lap.

Lauren. From Samuel.

A quick rip across the top. Or a fingernail under the seal. That's all it will take. Perhaps I will forgive. Forget. I look over to where it all happened. The floor. My pulse rises, but I'm not shaking like I thought I would be. No pictures come flying into my head, no memories scream at me. I thought this moment would be terrible, heartbreaking. But what I feel is hollowness. And as I hold Samuel's letter, I realise something huge: *I don't have to forgive him.*

The front gate creaks – Snap exiting the yard. The crappy thing is going to creak until the day it falls off its hinges. I jump up, about to chase after him, but there's the fire. I should put it out. Should make sure it's dampened. I stare at it for a moment, the flames reflecting the slow anger that burns at the edges of my heart. And, oh hell, an image of something terrible fills my mind. What if?

Snap is halfway down the street by the time I get outside. "Hey!" I call as quietly as I can. He turns and waits while I catch up. I give him Samuel's camera. "Don't sell it. I want you to have it."

He doesn't say anything, just smiles and carries it away.

Back at Mary's, I creep up to the front door, put the key in the lock and turn it as quietly as I can. The porch light flicks on. Crap. Mary opens the door. She doesn't look happy, standing there in her dressing gown with a crossword book in her hand. She must have got up to go to the loo then checked my room. She does that sometimes. I should have packed clothes or something into my bed, made it look as if I were still there.

"Where have you been?"

I stare, willing my brain to whizz up something believable. I've got nothing.

"I've been worried sick. I was about to call the police. Why didn't you tell me you were going out? And on a school night! Where did you go?"

My fist curls around the photo in my jacket pocket and an idea strikes me. I pull the picture out and show her. "I wanted a memento."

She squints. "You were across the road? At this hour?"

I shrug. "I couldn't help it. I ..."

"You silly girl. Come here." She hugs me. "Next time, tell me. We'll go together. Okay?"

"Okay."

She squeezes me again. "Now get to bed. I'll bring you a hot chocolate."

Mary's kind of alright.

———◦———

I'm woken by sirens and lights flashing outside my bedroom window. I push the blind aside and look out. The panic that hits my chest is a physical thump. NO. Tingles course through my body, fear running through every nerve. Two fire engines are parked across the road. Flames colour the sky red and orange while neighbours stand, hugging themselves, bathed in the fire's glow.

Thumping footsteps sound down the hall. Mary doesn't knock, just flings my door open. "Lauren! It's your house. What did you do?"

"I … nothing … I didn't do anything."

"You must have. It's burning."

I shake my head.

"Get dressed. Come out front."

She leaves me and hurries to join Fred on the porch.

I grab my phone, then drop it because my hands are shaking so much. I snatch it up again and Snap:

I screwed up. The house is burning.

I wait but there's no response. I text again:

Snap???? Wot do I do?

My phone rings.

"Oh god, Snap. They're going to kill me."

"Calm down, Kitten. What's happened?"

"The house. It's burning."

"Ah, shit. Does anyone know you were there?"

"Mary. She caught me coming home."

"She'll be okay, won't she? She's on your side?"

"I don't know. I told her before I didn't care if it burned down. She thinks I did it. Oh fuck. I'm in trouble, Snap. And there's a neighbour down the street. She saw me coming out of the house earlier today."

Snap is silent. I wait, dying inside.

"Pack a bag, Kitten. See you by the back fence in ten."

He hangs up. Is he serious? I can't. What about Mary and Fred? What about the police?

A text shoots through:

You can do it, Tiger!

18

Absconder

I'm so wishing I had my licence. Snap's a crap driver. And apart from being freezing because the freakin' heater doesn't work, I'm too scared to fall asleep in case Snap runs us off the road or hits a kangaroo. Okay, that would be unavoidable if some poor animal jumped out in front of us but ... "God, Snap. Stay on your own side of the road."

"You want to drive?"

"You know I can't."

"I'll teach you."

I'm not even going to answer that. The middle of the night, when we're running away, and I'm so strung out I could bite my whole fingers off, not just my nails, isn't the time or place for L plates. I squint as oncoming headlights grow into a glare, and a passing truck buffets our car. The smell of sheep poo filters through the car's air vents. It's something we should both be used to, living out here in the sticks, but we still scrunch our noses.

Further up the road, we approach Barry Coleman's hay teddy bear, and ... nooo ... as our headlights flash over the giant bales, they highlight a headless body. Oh god. Teddy's head has rolled off, and one of his arms is missing. I hope that's not an omen.

A couple more hours in, my brain is wandering into what-have-we-done territory. I refuse to go there, so I listen to my stomach instead. I'm not normally a fan of late-night snacks, so it must be the cold, the adrenaline, or my sugar levels. "I'd kill for a steamy, hot, salty dim sim. Did you bring anything to eat?" I ask.

Snap looks pleased with himself. "Back seat."

I lean between our seats, push aside our jackets and stuff, and spot a pink bag. I drag it onto my lap and look at it. "You're kidding me." It's a Hello Kitty backpack. Snap ignores me, eyes on the road for a change. "Is this from your grandma?" I ask. "Does she think you're a girl? Or does she know you're a fairy?" I laugh at my own stupid joke.

"Fuck you. I bought it on eBay. And that's *Princess* to you."

I snort.

"You want food or not?" he says.

"I do. And I love the backpack. It's gorgeous."

"You can borrow it, but it comes back to Mamma," he says.

I grin. "Really? Thanks." I zip open the bag. Inside is Samuel's camera and the packet of Tim Tams Snap took from the house. "Ha! Perfect."

There are five biscuits left. We munch through two each, and the fifth one sits in no-man's land, unclaimed. I keep glancing at it longingly.

"You can have it," Snaps says. "I've already eaten more than a lady should."

I savour the treat, slowly sucking the chocolate off the biscuit as I stare at the road ahead. Tiny glints sparkle back at us from the bitumen. Someone once told me those glints are spider eyes reflecting the headlights. I don't know if it's true, but I like the idea. I hope we're not squashing them.

My Tim Tam has been sucked dry of chocolate. I hold up the bare biscuit to Snap "You want?"

He's about to take it from me, then sees what I'm offering. "That's disgusting."

I laugh, shove half of it in my mouth and crunch. I think my panic is making me delirious.

⋘◆⋙

Bright light jars me. I crack open my eyelids, squinting as Snap pulls up to a petrol pump. It's one of those highway petrol stations with a big café and an even bigger area for truckers to park their rigs.

"What time is it?" I croak.

"Morning, Sleeping Beauty. Almost dawn. Hang tight, gotta refuel."

A blast of chill enters the car as Snap opens his door. I pull my jacket closer, shoving my hands into my pockets. Geez, and I thought it was cold inside the car. Something crinkles in my pocket, and when I realise what it is, I pull it out: Samuel's letter. I smooth it over my knees. I should throw it out. Should destroy it. But I don't. I pick up the Hello Kitty backpack and tuck the letter into an inside zip pocket.

Snap returns with giant cups of hot chocolate and bags of dim sims to warm our bellies. I could kiss him. When we're finished with our greasy, smelly, but oh-so-tasty junk food, he moves the car to a far corner of the parking lot so we can try to get a bit of sleep before hitting Melbourne. He says we're not far out, but nothing much will be open this time of the morning. "Take the back seat," he says. I don't object.

I pull my knees and arms into my body on the squeaky vinyl bench seat. Why didn't we think to bring a blanket or quilt, anything warm? The effect of the hot food wears off quickly, and our jackets aren't protection enough to stop us shivering. Somehow, just when I think there's no way in hell I'm going to get any sleep, I open my eyes to tall buildings, traffic and a brightening sky. So, this is Melbourne.

◆

"How long?" The guy at the hostel gives us a cursory once over. He's not who I'd expect to see for a receptionist. He's twenty maybe, wearing a t-shirt, sunnies on his head (for no apparent reason) and a black eye, which I can't help staring at. "Couple of weeks, maybe," Snap says. Reception guy hands us a clipboard with a form to fill out and reels off a list of do's and don'ts about the facilities, after-hours access, nearby transport and other stuff. I'm not really listening, still half-asleep, crusty from our night in the car. All I want is a hot shower and a bed. Any bed. And to know why he has a black eye.

"I'll need a credit card for security." The guy's tone says he's bored.

Snap ignores him, fills in half the form, then hands it back with a bunch of cash. The guy hesitates, though he doesn't seem like the kind of person who gives a toss. I'm right. He takes the cash.

Snap turns to me. "You don't mind sharing a room, do you? Save a few bucks."

I shake my head. Don't care.

The room is dingy, the towels ratty, but the two single beds look clean, and any soft surface is inviting at this moment. When I emerge from the shower, dressed in the only change of clothes I thought to bring with me – another pair of jeans and a t-shirt – Snap is sitting on his bed dialling his mobile.

I panic. "Who're you calling?"

"Granny," he mouths.

Of course. Who else would he know in Melbourne? And besides, his hand is shaking, his bottom lip caught between his teeth. After a few moments, he cuts the call.

"No luck?" I ask.

He throws the phone on the bed. "I'll try again later. Want some brekky? I saw a bakery a little way down the road."

"Sure."

"Croissants?"

As soon as Snap closes the door, I flop onto the other bed and close my eyes. Come at me, sleep. But no, the shower has woken me up, made me edgy. I stare at the ceiling and the single power-saving globe that hangs bare. There's nothing to make a hot drink with, nothing to make a toasted sandwich – we're supposed to use the communal kitchen. There's no hairdryer – my hair is knotted and wet. I think about turning on the television. I wonder if the fire has made it to the news. Probably not. What would city folk care?

And that's when this shivering takes over my body. Not the cold shivering from the car, but an unbearable, bone-jolting, muscle-tearing shivering. And a nausea that feels like my soul is being pulled out of my aching stomach. *What the hell am I doing here*? I want to go home. But there is no home. Not anymore.

I only just make it to the toilet before I vomit.

19

Interminable

My feet are killing me, as is the bore on the cash register next to mine. At every opportunity, she turns back to me and continues some drawn-out dilemma about the shitty job the salon down the road did on her SNS nails. I'm wondering why the hell she keeps going back there if it's so bad. And fork me ... no fuck me, how has she not done herself an injury, given the length of her talons?

I almost cry from relief when it hits seven and my shift is over, but my hand-over cashier is dawdling, chatting to a buddy instead of letting me go. *Come on, cow.* Can't she see I'm desperate to get out of here? And now, a customer is loading up my conveyor with a bucketload of groceries from her piled-high trolley. No way. I'm not doing this. I tally off the register, yank out the cash drawer – ignoring the customer's look of dismay – and stalk towards the lollygagging cashier, who's still yabbering. "All yours, sweetie." Maybe this is why no-one here likes me. Which is perfectly fine with me. Lollygagging. Ugh. Did I just think that? A word Samuel would have used? Shudder.

On the tram home, I tuck my carry bags with their meagre groceries under my feet, sit back, cross my arms and try not to think. But what else is there to do? Fall asleep and miss my stop? I pinch the skin on my inner arm, hoping the pain will distract me, wake me up. It doesn't. This is my life now. It's been weeks and Snap and I are still living in the hostel. Existing.

Back at the room, I unload our staples for the week: canned soup, pasta, rice, whatever veggies were cheap this week and bits and pieces from the quick-sale shelf – half-price broken biscuits usually meet Snap's budget approval. Once a week, we indulge in a cheap Thai binge. Tonight is not that night. It's three bean mix with potatoes and "Not Quite Right" misshapen carrots. I'm fine with that too – I'm not quite right myself. Besides, I don't have much of an appetite these days.

We could eat better, but Snap's adamant about not biting into his savings too much, so that we can afford to pay a bond on our own place once he gets a job. If he ever gets a job. He's trying though, and optimistic. Can't fault that. "Hang in there, Kitten. It'll happen. Don't worry." Getting through each day is enough to worry about, so I let him handle the money, and everything else, while the tedium of bleep bleep supermarket scanners slowly kills me.

I hope he feels like cooking tonight; I can't face carting this stuff down to the communal kitchen and fending off banal conversations with over-friendly students or needy travellers while I wait for things to boil – mainly my temper. Why am I so angry, shitty, tired all the time? I sleep like a shaggy dog – splayed, bedraggled, taking up more space than I should – every opportunity I get. I hardly get out of bed on weekends, except maybe to catch a movie – a once-a-month indulgence Snap allows, with bags of smuggled-in popcorn, cos it's cheaper to make at home. Irascible. I-r-a-s-c-i-b-l-e.

Geez, where did that come from? I haven't thought about Harry since forever.

I sink onto my bed, ohhhh the bliss. Close my eyelids, irresistibly heavy as magnets, and ... Damn it! That had better be Snap forgetting his keys, because if that's Dax from the room next door, asking if I know this week's internet password again, I'm gonna smack him. *Go to the office, you lazy little douchebag.*

Half asleep, I curse as I stumble over the shopping bags I left near the entrance, then wrench the door open. It's Dax, and the poor guy is almost cringing. He must have heard me swear. At least he didn't make a run for it back to his room, like he did once when Snap answered the door. I don't know where he's from or what he's doing here – don't want to get that personal – but in a fit of boredom, I once googled his name, and it said it was of Anglo-Germanic origin, meaning "badger', an animal related to the weasel. How apt.

"Really sorry to bother you," he says, "but I have a sprain, so can't walk far." He points to a bandage low on his stick-thin leg. This dude is one of those twenty-somethings who looks like a teen, eats his own body weight and never puts on an ounce. I've seen him wolf boxes of cereal in the kitchen. All that sugar. He shifts his balance, obviously in pain, and I imagine his leg snapping, twig-like. How do you even sprain a calf?

I sink against the door jamb. "Oh. That's ..." I can't put my words together. Brain could do with some of his sugar. "What's up?"

"I was wondering, if you're going to the kitchen soon, if you'd mind heating up my meal." He holds up a styrofoam cup of noodles, the kind that comes with a packet of artificial flavouring.

"Sure." I take it from him, tuck it against my chest, close the door and collapse back on the bed.

A while later, somebody shakes my shoulder. I open an eye to Snap holding a piece of paper in front of my face – some sort of a certificate. I roll over, half sit up. "What's that?"

"It's my ticket to a job."

"What?" I'm too tired for games.

"Sweetness, I got an RSA certificate so I can get a pub job." He holds a bottle of vodka in his other hand. "Time to practice."

"No thanks." I collapse back on my stomach.

"Come on, Kitten. Help me celebrate."

"Sleep."

"Pfft!"

"Food!"

"Sigh. So practical. Okay, I'll cook. What did you get?"

I drag an arm out from underneath me and point to the bags on the floor.

"Tch. So slovenly."

He picks up the bags, sorts through the items, then heads to the door with his arms full.

"Wait." I look around the bed, then push myself up and drag out the noodle cup from under my stomach, crushed. Shit. I toss it to Snap. "Throw that into the mix and make a serve for the dude next door, will you?"

He looks at me, quizzical.

"Please."

He shakes his head and leaves.

———⋅◆⋅———

Snap does what he says he's going to do and lands a bartender job at a pub one suburb away. Brunswick. By January, we've saved enough for a bond plus three months' rent on a crumbly old seventies apartment. I'm in awe. I'd probably be living on the street by now if it weren't for him. He even still has most of his savings in case everything falls in a heap. Which is lucky for us because his grandmother hasn't returned his calls, and he's stopped trying. Cow.

Today we're op-shopping for furniture. He vetos everything I point to, so I give up and drag along behind, nodding in sulky agreement with what he chooses instead, even though I really don't care. It's hard to care about anything these days. Except sleep.

I think about getting a better job. Maybe I should go back to school. I think I'd like to teach. Kids. Young ones. I'd like to be someone they could talk to, someone safe for them. Meh. Study would be too much effort. Too much energy. Thinking is all I do. When I'm awake.

Snap buys a laptop, and I waste hours surfing, wanting to connect with someone. Anyone. But I'm afraid to get on Facebook. Someone might see me. I guess I could use a fake profile. How ironic.

———◄O►———

February. I turn seventeen in a couple of weeks, and I'm so regretting I let it slip to Snap because he wants a party. "No. Absolutely not." I'm not going to be having any more birthday parties. Ever. But I can't tell him that, or why I'm dreading the date approaching.

I sip my coffee, made with the new Aldi pod machine he's bought – along with every other appliance in our kitchen. I've contributed a big fat zero; I'm only just covering my share of the rent and living expenses.

"Come on. It'll be a joint party. I missed my last birthday cos we were saving."

"I don't have any friends to invite." It's true. I'm so boring, nobody invites me anywhere, to anything. Not that I'd go. Hell, no. Snap and I are opposite like that; he has a life, he likes his work, he makes friends easily, he goes to the gym and out for dinner. I don't. I miss my mum. I miss having a home. A real one.

"What about some of the people from your work?"

I nearly spit my coffee.

"Fine! I'll invite a few people from *my* work. They're fun. You'll like them," he says. "Come on-n-n-n-n. Let's cheer you up."

Surrogate friends. Even more depressing. Sigh. How does he stand me?

When the day comes, I help him clean up the apartment, blow up balloons, hang stupid streamers. He's even bought me a cake and makes me stand in front of it while he takes a picture with Samuel's camera – he's figured out to how to use it, and I grudgingly agree he's taken a good shot, though it would be even better if he cropped my sorry self out of it. But by afternoon, I make myself scarce. I walk, for miles, find a library to hide in, a movie to see, then another, hang around McDonald's, and don't come home until daybreak. And he doesn't even hate me for it.

20

Transmogrification

July. It's already been a year, but it feels like a lifetime. I've done nothing; I'm still wallowing at my cash register, while Snap now has two jobs: bartending and running a male phone-sex line from his bedroom. Holy crap, his father would have an aneurism. When he suggests I do the same, I shut him down. No discussion. "Well, find something you actually like," he says. "Something that makes you want to get out of bed." I tell him where to go. Thank god he loves me.

Today, however, I've been in bed for forty hours, it's midday, my blinds are shut, and I think my room smells.

"Get the fuck up!"

What the? It's not so much the sudden stab of light as he yanks the blinds open that shocks me, but ... Snap doesn't swear. Hardly.

"Have a shower and get dressed. You've got a job interview."

"What? Where?"

"The pub."

"I don't want it. I'm not even legal." I also don't trust myself around alcohol. I've been getting a taste for vodka: in my orange juice, my apple juice, my iced tea, my water bottle. Hell, a straight swig or two from the bottle before I leave for work will do – paired with a couple of Panadol – and I'm set. Tame, sure, but it's only downhill from here, right?

"You'll start in the bistro. The pay will be better, and you can study for your VCE in your down time. You don't even have to get your arse to class."

"Leave me al-o-o-o-ne."

He grabs my doona and pulls it off me. "You can do it online. We'll do it together," he says.

"Really?" I grumble, sitting on the edge of my bed now. Good thing I have a t-shirt and undies on. "You want to live in each other's pockets, study and work together, too?"

"It'll be fun."

I seriously doubt it, but it might be better than the supermarket. "I don't know anything about pub work."

"I'll teach you. Bob won't care. You've got boobs."

Sigh. I'm running out of objections.

"You'll get tips," he adds

"Fine! They better be big ones."

"Bigger the better," he says. "You just gotta do this." He pushes up non-existent boobs.

I blush. "That's not happening."

He picks up a half bottle of vodka from the floor, beside my bed. "Step one, Kitten. Education. How to handle your booze. You're officially on rations."

He turns out to be right: Bob doesn't ask questions, doesn't look past my low-cut t-shirt, my too-heavy lipstick, both of which Snap assures me I'll only have to wear the once. The pay is better, cash, but I don't get super or sick leave since I'm off the books. There's music, there's people having fun, and after a couple of months, I grudgingly start to relax. Even crack a smile now and then, though I'm careful because Bob is, as Snap warns, a perv.

⸺⋄⸺

The bistro is empty this time of afternoon, the in-between breathing moment when Caesar salad lunchers have abandoned their tables to crumbs and coffee-dregged cups. A moment, where my mind can drift as sunlight through the orange glass-brick windows softens and hushes the room, where I can almost imagine my life is normal while I push a damp cloth over tables, refill salt and pepper shakers, top up drink coaster stacks. Someone's left a lump of chewing gum on the side of this table. Gross. At least stick it underneath.

Normal. My life is normal now. I have a place to live, a job, a good friend. A lot more than some people have. I'm safe. There's just one thing ... I stop work to pull out a piece of paper from my jeans pocket. I've looked at the phone number on it so often, I should know it by heart now, but I don't. My mind doesn't want to retain it – Mum's nursing home. I've been thinking about this for weeks, months. My need is two-fold: Mum and Mary. I feel cruel having left it this long but ... reasons. Still, what if Mum's died and I have no idea? But there's the fire, the police. And Mary, I just know she'll beg me to come home. This is my home now.

I've figured it out though: if I call from the payphone here, ask about Mum, leave a message for Mary – say that I'm okay and not to worry – it'll be safe won't it? Short, sharp, and Mary won't have a number to trace. That'll work, won't it? I can't see any reason why not.

I bite my lip, squeeze the cloth in my hand, then throw it onto the table. Do it. Just get it done. Don't think.

I dial wrong at first and have to start again, focusing harder on the paper trembling in my hand. The woman who answers wants to know who I am.

"Delia's daughter. Lauren." The home isn't that big. She'll know Mum.

Her "Oh" is loaded, but I can't tell if it's judgement, accusation or surprise. Eighteen months is a long time to not check on your last living relative. "Give me a minute," she says.

I nearly hang up in panic. What if she knows? Remembers what happened? What if she's telling someone she has a criminal on the line, right now?

"Delia's fine. Her dementia is progressing slowly, but she's still active and eating well."

My throat is tight, but I manage a chuckle. "Mum was never one to hold back when there's food around."

"Did you want to see if she can come—"

"Could I ... could I leave a message for Mary? Mary Worthington. She's a volunteer there."

"We don't usually—"

"Please. It's important. I don't know her home number, and I'm guessing you're not going to give it to me?"

She baulks at this, then relents.

"Tell her I'm okay. That she doesn't have to worry. Okay?"

"I'm just writing this down. Did you want to leave a—"

"I have to go. Sorry." I hang up.

I don't move for a minute, just breathe. Eventually, I shrug the stiffness from my shoulders, then lower my head and close my eyes, searching for some sort of emotion. I did it. I did the thing. I should be guilt-free now, but I'm not sure what I feel. No lightness of relief, just numbness. I'll run with that; maybe it'll hit me later. I've become good at holding back, even proud of it.

I head back to the bistro, pick up my cloth and continue cleaning. And as I move, I become more fluid, easier in myself. Lighter. I do feel lighter. Huh. It's a nice feeling. I'd forgotten it.

As I approach the table closest to the karaoke stage, the red light on the machine catches my eye. Bob must have left it on. I hop up on the beer-infested carpeted riser and glance over the mixer. Where's the power button? I push aside the stack of printed song lists, then stop to consider them. I wonder? Flick, flick. P. Q. R. S. I breathe in sharply, run my finger over the song title, maybe to feel if it's real.

I don't know what overtakes me, but I turn to the karaoke machine and press the touchscreen, scroll through the options. I'm not going to sing it, just listen while I clean.

Press.

I close my eyes as the first notes start, that simple, sweet, happy piano, the rhythm of two notes, repeating, making me want to sway. And I can't help it; I pick up the microphone. I still know the words by heart – the girl who makes him dizzy, who's a flower in a sidewalk crack, who makes him ... smile. And I do. And my heart does. Remembering something good at last, something bittersweet.

I'm halfway through the song before I notice Bob, Snap and the cook gathered in the kitchen doorway, grinning at me. I falter, but they yell at me to keep going.

And I do.

Sneak peek at book 2

Here's a sneak peek at chapter 1 of book 2:

How You Found Me.

Bad things happen on my birthdays. Like this boozy mob. They look as though they're enjoying a lynching: mine. Talk about sweating it. Whoever invented the karaoke machine must have had ancestors who cheered at public executions, back when Marie Antoinette fictitiously told everyone to eat cake. I'm supposed to be geeing-up this Fitzroy pub crowd, not that they need it.

Oh god. It might seem as though I'm pulling a dance move, but I'm just trying to avoid getting my heels caught in the gap between the stage risers. With each shift, I have to peel the soles of my boots off the sticky carpet.

I'm staring at lyrics that make me think Justin Bieber and Rihanna are conspiring to give birth to a love child: *baby, baby, baby; yeah, yeah, yeah; give it to me, give it to me.* The poor excuse for a song breaks into a rap section, and I stand with one hand in my jeans pocket, a dork waiting for the torture to end.

Bob picked the song. "The punters'll go for it," he said.

They're not. They're holding their beers aloft, laughing at my piss-poor effort to get the party started. My face is burning, and it's not from the fuggy heat of the bar. It's because I *can* sing. Properly. Just not this rubbish. Let me die. Now.

It's a vocal limp to the end of the track before I shove the microphone back onto the stand. Bob collects several scraps of paper – scribbled song requests from Elvis and Beyoncé wannabes who think they can do a better job than me. Yeah, everyone can sing when they're drunk. He lumbers onto the stage. "Give it up for Lauren, our very own Rihanna!" The applause is surprisingly enthusiastic, but I'm sure it's more about getting me off the stage. I'm seriously happy to comply.

Safe behind the bar, I wrap my apron around my waist. It's back to pulling beers, cracking UDLs and batting off puns based on my crap performance. Suddenly, it's comedy hour:

"Hey, love. You should eat more tuna! Get it? Tune-er?"

"I'll tune her if she likes!"

Hilarious. As I bend to the lower fridge to grab a pear cider for the chick in the tight skirt and even tighter t-shirt, some dickhead throws a bottle top at my butt. I spring upright, lean across the bar and threaten him with the prong of a corkscrew.

"Not cool," I hiss.

The guy holds both hands up, claiming innocence while his mate beside him guffaws. In the seconds it takes me to realise I've chosen the wrong perpetrator, guffawing guy's shoulder is grasped by a tall blond dude.

"Apologise," the dude says.

"Sorry, love."

I'm thrown, unsure whether to tell the blond dude thanks very much, but I can look after myself, or to smile my gratitude. I choose grateful. Decency is rare in this bar. Heckle and Jeckle take their beers elsewhere while the dude sits at the bar.

"Hey, birthday girl."

I swear my heart stops for a second. No-one but Snap knows it's my birthday, that I'm finally legal. I look closer and recognition hits me: the grey eyes, the wide smile, the face – now hidden behind a mass of hipster beard. His hair is longer and tied back in a loose ponytail.

"Spell *serendipitous,*" he says.

"Harry?"

For a second, I have this insane reflex to turn and run.

An easy way to support your favourite authors

Did you know that leaving a review on Goodreads or Amazon will make you 10% more attractive? It's also one of the quickest and easiest ways to show your support for an author. A single sentence from you (it doesn't need to be an essay) helps authors be seen by other readers.

So while you're here, why don't you pop onto one of the sites now and leave a quick review? I would be super grateful you made the effort.

Acknowledgements

Since this is my first book and took six years to write, I have a heck of a lot people to thank. So, you can swoosh straight past these acknowledgements if you weren't involved.

Where to start? This feels like sorting out a seating plan at a wedding – who do I sit upfront, in the middle, up the back? Hell, I'm just going to toss names up the in air and see where they land.

Chris Collins, my supplier of cat food, sanity and mortgage payments. One day, I'll upgrade your car and buy us that dream home in Port Douglas. Love you and our bunnies to bits. You are my rock.

My RMIT PWE buddies who have stayed in touch via our Chicken Writers group and become the most amazing and generous of friends: Kathryn Moore, Jo Burnell, Connie Spanos, Ara Sarafian. You all give an abundance of love, time and patience. You are a lesson in endurance when I rail against feedback. You are my personal cheer squad who support me as I whine, wine and write. You must all be a little crazy.

Nikki Bielinski, Sylvia Goudie, Adam VanLangenberg, Tim Byrne, Deborah Vanderwerp, Hutch Stevens. Each of you have helped me along this bumpy ride, if not on this book, then as a developing writer.

Nicole Hayes thank you for your friendship, generosity and years of guidance in your workshops, and for taking time out from your crazy busy schedule to read my manuscript. Melissa Manning bless you for your endless encouragement, belief, support and advice when you were so deep in your own work and should have been focused on yourself.

RMIT and TAFE PWE tutors and classmates. Thank you for your knowledge and generosity when I returned to study, vulnerable and not knowing how much I didn't know.

Stuart Reedy and the Phoenix Park Writers group, for the camaraderie and endless weeks, years of workshopping. Stuart, I could always feel you believed in me. Marisa Pintado of Hardie Grant and Melanie Ostell, you probably don't know how much your time and encouragement meant.

Sally Hetherington thanks for your help with the original artwork way back when. Sorry, I couldn't keep my fingers out, but you know you love me. Elizabeth Stevens, you are a star. Thanks for the selfpub hand-holding.

Ari Gershevitch, Geraldine Stallard, Ruth Van Gramberg, Sally Odgers, Theresa Bonn, Lana Collins, Joe Pryke, for your fresh eyes on my manuscript in its various forms.

Ena Makaus, for getting me hooked on writing in the first place. Who knew where that first TAFE class, "Find Your Inner Voice", would lead? Susan Manderson for pushing me to jump when I doubted myself.

My AJC Publishing editors, beta reading team, and editing mentor Wendy Monaghan: without your professionalism and dedication, I wouldn't have the time to write at all.

And finally, me, because I freakin' did it. Now where's the wine and chocolate?

About the author

Cienna Collins is an Australian author of domestic noir suspense. Her books were longlisted for the QWC Adaptable film and television program and won a Publishable mentorship. Cienna was also awarded a placement at Hardcopy – a national professional development program for writers. Her short stories have won numerous awards and have been read on Radio Queensland.

Cienna has an Associate Degree in Professional Writing & Editing and runs a successful book editing and audiobook production business, AJC Publishing. Previous to this, Cienna had an eclectic career including managing commercial mortgages, working in a legal tribunal and fronting her own function band for over twenty years.

A previous devotee of adrenaline sports, including bungee jumping, skydiving, parasailing, sky-walking, sky-jumping and volcano climbing, Cienna is now happy to be settled at home in Melbourne with her hubby and two fur-kids, writing her adventures instead of living dangerously.

Stay in Touch
Join Cienna's mailing list: https://ciennacollins.com